HORNBI

Fenella Bass

APS BOOKS

APS Books,
4 Oakleigh Road,
Stourbridge,
West Midlands,
DY8 2JX

APS Books is a subsidiary of
the APS Publications imprint

www.andrewsparke.com

ISBN 9781789960440

Yesterday upon the stair,
I met a man who wasn't there,
He wasn't there again today,
I wish, I wish he'd go away.

Chapter One

THE first thing to break through to her consciousness was the complete silence, or should that be the total lack of noise? Opening her eyes cautiously, she looked around the unfamiliar room and wondered for a split second where the hell she was. Her gaze alighting on the familiar sight of her two Italian Greyhounds, jolted her brain into remembrance. Of course, she was in her new home. Stretching gently, so as not to wake them, she reflected on the previous day. Moving day; fairly traumatic but could have been worse. At least she was here, the bedroom was reasonably straight and if she closed her mind to the accumulation of boxes residing in the room she had designated her study then the rest of the cottage wasn't too bad either!

It was so quiet. She was used to waking in her London flat to the constant sound of street noise. This was just so totally different.

The dogs, alerted by her movement, started to stretch and wag their tails.

'Okay boys, time to get up I think.'

She was rewarded with much wriggling and tail wagging as the three of them jumped out of bed. *I must get a rug for this room*, she thought as their feet and paws hit the bare, varnished floorboards. Gingerly, she made her way down the narrow stairs that led directly into the kitchen. Looking around she took in and appreciated the cupboards finished in distressed blue paint, the appliances which the previous owner had kindly included in the sale and last but not least the beautiful view of the garden and the Fens beyond. Dennis would have loved it, she found herself thinking and then quickly blocked this from her mind. Her husband's sudden and totally unexpected death at the age of thirty-eight was something she was not ready to dwell upon, especially not on this, the very first day of her new life.

'Breakfast, boys I think,' she addressed the pair of hopeful faces gazing up at her, 'but a quick trip outside for you both first.'

She opened the back door and watched as two figures hurtled outside into the walled garden and found two shrubs on which to relieve themselves before dashing back in to sit hopefully in front of her. Grabbing their bowls, she located the tinned food they had for breakfast and transferred some. Before she could even put the bowls on the floor two noses were nudging to see what she had. She filled the kettle and sat down at the pine kitchen table whilst waiting for it to boil. It looked as if it was going to be a beautiful day. The sun was already breaking through and it felt pleasantly warm. She looked in two or three cupboards before she managed to locate the cafetière and once she had filled it, she took it and her favourite mug outside and sat at the outdoor table which was situated under a kind of pergola at the side of the garden. The dogs came out and began to nose around the garden.

Despite her determination not to think about Dennis, she found her mind wandering back to their life together in Highgate, which had culminated in his death two days before Christmas the previous year.

He'd gone out to Muswell Hill for some last-minute Christmas shopping, totally unaware that what awaited him was a drunk driver, who had mounted the pavement, killing him instantly.

She had been at home when the two police officers called.

'Mrs McClean? Mrs Magda McClean?' the male officer asked and it was a few moments before she collected herself enough to answer, fearing to hear what their presence on the doorstep signified.

'Yes, I am,' she finally managed by way of a response.

'May we come in? I'm afraid we have upsetting news for you.' The female officer spoke for the first time.

She led them into the lounge which overlooked Highgate Woods and felt as if you were living amongst the treetops. The three of them sat down and very gently the two officers guided her through what had happened.

'We're here to take you down to the hospital, love,' the male officer told her and for one brief, joyful moment she found herself thinking, *well he must be alive if they want me to visit him in hospital*, before the dreadful reality of what they really meant penetrated through.

'Have you got someone who can come with us love?' She shook her head,

'No, not really. Everyone I know is at work.' Very gently the female officer, who had identified herself as Karen took her elbow to help her up from the settee.

'It's the Whittington.'

In a daze, she fumbled for her handbag and coat and followed numbly down the stairs and out to the waiting car. To this day she was unable to recall anything about that nightmare journey or even what followed.

When they pulled back the curtain that obscured the glass viewing screen, she did not immediately recognise her husband lying there. He looked like an effigy or statue not something living, which, of course, he no longer was. She nodded identification, unable to coax any sound from her vocal chords.

'Thank you, Mrs McClean.'

The male officer, she never did get to find out his name, guided her back outside once again to the waiting car.

What followed, was if anything, even worse. For the first day she could not even bring herself to ring her mother-in-law in Ireland. Dennis' mother had never approved of her son's choice of wife, mainly because Magda was not Catholic. She and Dennis' sister had attended the wedding reluctantly, but the ice between them and his new bride had never thawed. So much so, that Dennis, a gentle and peaceful soul, used to visit them alone, at least once a year.

Finally, Magda managed to rouse herself sufficiently to make the call. Margaret screamed and screamed down the phone, before handing the receiver to Roisin who told Magda that they would be in touch, before summarily hanging up.

The funeral had brought about no form of reconciliation although Magda had given in to Margaret's insistence that her only son be buried rather than cremated, which she had deemed as being sinful. The two McCleans had stood apart from all the rest of the congregation at the graveside, leaving Magda to stand with only her friends for support, her parents having both died before she and Dennis had even met. Never in her life had she felt more alone as she stood and watched, while the rain shed its silent tears over the grave of a lovely, kind man.

That feeling of total aloneness had never gone far away. She had continued to work and eat, but had found sleep almost impossible. It was her downstairs neighbour, an elderly lady of over eighty who had suggested she get herself a dog.

'It will be company for you,' Beth encouraged 'and you can use my garden. In fact, I'll go up and let it out for you while you're at work.'

Magda was unsure, but Beth was so insistent, raising the subject more or less every time Magda saw her, that one Sunday afternoon in late February, she and the elderly lady drove to Potters Bar to the RSPCA. As she looked around at all the sad faces and eyes that seemed to mirror just how she was feeling, Magda felt she could not possibly take on the responsibility of a dog. However, in one of the kennels a bundle of what looked like soft blue grey satin morphed into two little elegant beings who approached the door tentatively and stood shivering before coming forward hesitantly for Beth to pat one. Magda felt too overawed to do so, but instantly fell in love.

'They're whippets I think,' Beth informed her.

'They're beautiful.' Magda felt she shouldn't breathe too hard for fear of scaring them.

'Come on.' Beth took her arm firmly. 'Let's go and see about them.' Magda found herself being propelled towards the reception area.

'We want to ask about the whippets.' Beth told the surprised looking young man behind the counter.

'Whippets? We don't currently have any whippets at the moment, I'm afraid.'

'Yes you do, young man, the two in the last but one cage.'

'Oh, they're not whippets. They're Italian Greyhounds. They're two brothers, two years old. Their owner died, sadly. We need to home them together, as they've never been apart, so we wouldn't consider separating them I'm afraid.' He smiled reluctantly at Beth. Magda knew what was coming almost before Beth turned to her.

'There you are, you have to take them; their owner died.' After much filling in of forms and a home check Magda found herself the proud owner of the two little dogs, whom she named *Aymes* and *Rollins*.

And it was down to the two little dogs that she had found her new home.

One Sunday, towards the end of April, feeling cooped up in the flat, she had loaded them all into the car and set off down the A10 towards Hertfordshire. She continued to drive on into Cambridgeshire before stopping to allow the dogs a comfort break. She had absolutely no idea where she was and when they took off down a track next to a river, she panicked. Shouting and chasing after them, she cursed herself for being so stupid as to let them off the lead in a strange place. After what seemed like hours, but was probably only a few minutes, she spotted a little lane which turned off from the main path. Following that whilst repeatedly calling their names, she came to a small clearing with four small detached cottages built in an arc around a central piece of lawn. Outside one of the cottages, tails wagging stood the two dogs.

'Oh you naughty boys' Magda, bent down to secure their leads, whilst giving both of them a stroke. As she straightened, she noticed that there was a rather lop sided *For Sale* sign outside the one at the far end. Intrigued she wandered over and, opening the rickety gate, went into the small but beautiful front garden. Later, she was to tell friends that she fell in love instantly with what was to become her future home.

The garden was overgrown but the cottage looked in good repair. It had what looked like a new roof and double-glazed windows, with small panes of glass very much in keeping with the style of the cottage. The stonework was of a yellow, buttery coloured stone, with a newly painted black front door.

Wondering whether she had the courage to knock on the door, but unable to resist the lure, she did so hesitantly and an immense feeling of disappointment overwhelmed her when there was no reply. Searching in her handbag for a pen and paper on which to jot down the number of the estate agent, she almost tripped over something raised on the edge of the path. It seemed to be a little mound of some kind with a beautiful flowering shrub planted in the centre. Underneath was what looked like a stone with something written on it. Closer inspection revealed what she thought might be a name *Amoretta*.

There was no denying that something about the whole place seemed to call to her and for the first time since Dennis' death she felt as if there could be a slight ray of light poking through the heavy clouds which had descended since that awful day in December. Reluctantly she turned around and walked out through the gate, but felt compelled to take one final look at the property before returning to the car.

Once back, she searched in her bag for her mobile and with little or no hesitation dialled the estate agent's number. They won't be there on a Sunday, she admonished herself and a feeling akin to panic took over, only relieved when a voice answered.

'Hello, I'm ringing about the cottage in...' Oh God, she realised suddenly, she had no idea where she or the cottage was. 'About the cottage, it's...er...off a lane off a road somewhere just off the A10. It's um near a small river. It's got yellow walls and a lovely garden, and there are three others in like a horseshoe-shape and...' She was aware she was babbling.

'Hold on a minute,' the voice at the other end bade her. 'I'm just a Sunday person, but my boss will know. I'll just give him a quick call.'

A few minutes later he was back on the line.

'He's sure you mean *Hornbeams*. It's still on the market. The owner died and her grandson inherited the property. He had it refurbished but he lives abroad so wants to sell.'

He quoted a figure, which to Magda, used to London prices sounded ridiculously cheap.

'Are you sure?'

'Yes, but you could probably beat him down with an offer, he's very keen to sell. I could show you round if you like. We're not too far away.' He named a town she hadn't heard of.

'That would be amazing, I live in London. I'm only here for the afternoon.'

'Shall we say two thirty?'

Checking her watch, she saw it was one-forty-five. 'Ideal, thank you, shall I meet you outside?'

'Absolutely, my name's Rob and I'll be at Hornbeams then at two-thirty'.

Thanking him, she disconnected and sat looking about at the surrounding countryside. It was flat, and rather marshy but she felt at home. She liked the feeling of the wide-open space; it made her feel free. The day wasn't particularly sunny or warm but it didn't feel depressing like London did when the weather was bad. She left the car and she and the dogs walked leisurely along the river bank until it was time to return to meet with the agent.

Rob turned out to be young. He was waiting, as promised, on the path outside the front door. He had the usual clipboard and estate agent paraphernalia with him and he handed her a printed set of particulars for the property. He located the front door key and inserting it into the lock he pushed open the front door. The cottage was small, but there was a lovely feel to the living room which was square, with a window on either side of the front door. It had a built-in recess on one wall and Magda could imagine putting some of her beloved books there. Meanwhile Rob had opened another door off to the side which Magda hadn't noticed, revealing another small room with a window to the side of the cottage. A study, Magda thought breathlessly. They continued on into the kitchen, which housed the stairs to the upper storey.

'It's the vendor's son or grandson, who owns it. He had the roof replaced and a new boiler fitted.' Rob consulted his clipboard. 'He's including all the fixtures and white goods, so you can just move in, with very little fuss.'

Climbing the stairs, which were rather steep, Magda had a strange sensation, like deja-vu. She ignored it and followed in Rob's wake to the first floor. There were two bedrooms and a bathroom with a shower stall as well as a bath. Magda knew immediately which room she would choose to sleep in if she went ahead and bought the place. It overlooked the garden at the back, from two lovely windows set low in the wall underneath one of which was a window seat. Rob was still burbling on and Magda gently silenced him with a raised hand.

'It's lovely, beautiful and I am going to buy it.' The words came almost unbidden.

'He'll take an offer I'm sure.' Once again Magda gently raised a hand.

'It's ok, I'll meet the asking price.'

Rob looked stunned.

'I've only been doing this job a month.' He stammered, apropos of nothing.

His youth suddenly made Magda feel old and weary. 'You're doing fine.' She reassured him.

Chapter Two

AFTER her meeting with Rob she had driven home feeling very excited. The following day she went into a local Estate Agency and arranged for them to look over her property. They arrived that afternoon and their valuation was shockingly high.

'Are you sure?'

'Of course.' The agent smiled rather condescendingly Magda thought. 'It's in a prime location, has two bedrooms and is a conversion which means a lot of the original features are still in place. Believe me people love this sort of thing, they'll be queuing up to put in an offer.'

Despite her dislike of him, the agent had been proved right and within two week's she had a firm buyer. Now she had to deal with telling Beth. The elderly lady had become one of the few people Magda felt comfortable with since Dennis' death. They had spent many evenings together having bonded over the little dogs. True to her word Beth had come in to let them out when Magda was at work. Leaving Beth would be a wrench for both of them she had no doubt about it. The evening after her offer on the cottage was accepted, Magda went downstairs with a box of chocolates and a bottle of Elderflower cordial which Beth loved.

'Come in my dear, how lovely to see you. I must say you are looking well too. You look as if a weight has been lifted. I let the boys out earlier, they were fine and did everything they needed to. I still have a bit of difficulty telling them apart, but I think it was Rollins, came in and sat on my lap, so sweet.'

Magda felt dreadful, however was she going to break the news? She waited until Beth had poured them both a drink before launching into what she had to say. When putting the flat on the market she had eschewed a *For Sale* sign as she hadn't wanted to upset Beth.

'I've got some news. Good news and I hope you will think so too.'

'Go ahead my dear, I'm intrigued.' Beth patted her hand encouragingly.

'I've bought a house, well a cottage really, but it's in Cambridgeshire.' She stopped breathlessly.

'Aaah. So that's who that young man was I saw coming up here a few times. He always had someone different with him so was sure he wasn't simply a friend. Of course it's good news. It will be a fresh start after all you've been through. Mind you, I'm going to miss you like mad, but my dear girl, this is your life, the best time of your life. You need to be able to move on and start again. Isn't that what you would tell your patients?' Beth knew Magda was a counsellor, working for the local health service. However, as it was the NHS she had never grasped that *patients* were now referred to as *clients*. Her old-fashioned attitude was what had charmed both Magda and Dennis when they first moved into their flat.

'Yes, that's exactly what I should be saying, but I will never, ever be able to thank you for all you've done for me since I lost Dennis.' Beth patted her hand again.

'Believe me my dear it was the least I could do. Such a lovely man and you were such a lovely couple together. When I had this house converted into two flats, I was very apprehensive. I knew I couldn't manage the house alone when Arthur died but couldn't bring myself to leave here either. It had been our home since we first married. As you know we were never blessed with children, so the house and garden became like a child to us. I was so thrilled when you bought the flat. You were the type of people I had longed for and never believed I would be lucky enough to get. You never made noise, you were kind, polite, friendly and considerate. I will miss you no end but we can chat on the phone and you never know, I might even be able to rouse these old bones to come and see you. Cambridge isn't the other side of the world you know!' Beth's eyes twinkled as she said this.

'Oh, it's not actually Cambridge. It's in the Fens, near Ramsey. But I would absolutely love it if you came. You could stay…stay as long as you like. In fact, I could come and get you and then bring you back when you've had enough.'

'Of course I'll come. I look forward to it. Now tell me who am I going to have for new neighbours and don't spare me, I want the truth.'

'Actually, I think you'll like them. The husband's American and the lady is English. They're probably my age or maybe slightly older. He works in an American bank in the city and she's a physiotherapist. They don't have any children, or pets as far as I know. They are pleased not to have the worry of a garden and they said they will leave the flat exactly as it is.'

Dennis, as a freelance illustrator, had made a wonderful job of the interior and Magda had been thrilled when they said they didn't want to change anything. She hoped she would be able to work some of his magic on the new cottage. It didn't need anything doing but was completely colour neutral and the first thing she was going to do was paint her bedroom the same pale mauve as the one in the flat.

Beth said she liked the sound of the Axelrods but reassured Magda that however nice they were, they would never be as nice as herself and Dennis.

'I'm really going to miss those little dogs, but a lovely big garden and country walks are just what they need. What do you plan to do about working?'

'Well, I'm very well set for money, so nothing for the foreseeable future. I'm going to settle in, maybe take a year and then look for some part-time work. I haven't felt I've really been present for my clients since I lost Dennis. His life insurance and the extra money from the flat will allow me time to come to terms with everything. I want to work again, as I love it, but when I feel ready.'

'Absolutely; very wise. You'll know when the time is right, I know.'

When she left some hours later and went back up to her flat, she reflected on how much she was going to miss her neighbour. Clipping the dogs' leads on, she went downstairs and across the road to the woods. Despite the dark she wasn't frightened. She had never lived anywhere else but London and felt totally at home there. *I hope I feel as at home in the new place* she thought as, the dogs having done what they needed for the night, she made her way back to the flat.

Moving day arrived. It went fairly well. She was lucky with the June weather. Beth had given her a beautiful Hydrangea plant for the new garden and a box of treats for the dogs. Her friends from both work and ones she had known since school threw a going away dinner for her. Her oldest and best friend Lydia was going to come down and visit when Magda felt settled enough.

Beth too promised that she would not renege on her promise to come and visit. 'If you feel at all lonely, give me a ring.' She told Magda as she waved her off, behind the removal van.

They made good time and by six-thirty in the evening everything was more or less in place. The two removal men were friendly and cheerful and appreciated all the cups of tea Magda made for them. They drove off with a cheery wave, leaving her to face the first night in her new home.

Now on the first morning she looked around the garden and thought about how she might spend the day. She could be sensible and unpack all her books or she could take the dogs out and explore. The lure of the fine weather proved too much and after a shower, she dressed, got the dogs and walked outside. She wandered down by the river. It was so quiet. It was also very flat, but she loved the feeling of space and distance. The dogs, when she let them off, went playing and splashing through the reed beds. Every now and then they ran back to make sure she was there before rushing off again. When she looked at her watch, she was amazed to see that it had gone midday. Calling the dogs, she set off back home.

As she got into the little cul-de-sac, she saw a lady working in the garden of the cottage on the other end of the terrace from hers.

'Hello, you must be the new girl.' The lady, who was in her fifties gave Magda a cheery wave, beckoning her over. 'I'm Janette; Janette Brooker.' She removed a gardening glove and offered Magda her hand to shake.

'Magda, Magda McClean and yes I'm the new neighbour.'

'Thought so. I was saying to Max I wondered what you'd be like. Have you met him yet, Max? He lives in the cottage next to you.' Magda shook her head.

'No. I only arrived yesterday, you're the first person I've met.'

'Oh, we're a pretty good bunch here. There's me and Max and now you and then there's the Griffiths. They're a holiday home. Not here all the time. They grace us with their presence every now and again. She's lovely; not so sure about the husband; bit of a bastard I'd have to say and the kids, well! Teenagers, which says it all.'

Magda had to smile.

'Come on in and have a coffee. Give me a good excuse to stop working in the garden, which I hate by the way.'

Magda wanted to refuse. She didn't feel able to go into her life story, especially the part about Dennis, but there was something so welcoming about Janette, that she didn't want to offend her with a refusal. She hesitated for a minute.

'I've got these two.' She indicated the dogs, standing patiently next to her.

'That's fine, bring them, I love dogs. We'll sit in the garden if you prefer. They're skinny little things. You sure you feed them enough?'

Magda hadn't missed the roguish twinkle in Janette's eye. Laughing, she said she did.

'I know. They're whippets, aren't they? Too small to be greyhounds.'

'Actually, they're Italian Greyhounds.'

'My goodness and so pretty and delicate looking. Here boys. What are their names?'

'Aymes and Rollins. I named them after my late husband's favourite cricketers.' There it was out, she'd said it, my late husband.

Rather disconcertingly Janette moved over and put an arm around

Magda's shoulders. 'You dear girl, so young to be widowed. I'm really sorry.' She moved away, as if uncertain she should have been so forward, which made Magda like her even more.

'Thank you. It was very sudden, an accident. This is supposed to be my fresh start.'

'Well you've made a good choice. Come on in and let's have that coffee.'

Magda followed Janette through her cottage. It was similar to her own. But Janette had put her own stamp on it, making it the home Magda hoped she might make of her own. She let Janette escort her into the garden and settle, whilst she went back in to make the coffee.

Janette reappeared bearing a tray with a large cafetière, mugs, sugar bowl, biscuits and a large bowl of water for the dogs. 'I thought these two might need a drink and feel free to give them as many biscuits as you like. There are plenty more inside. I can't resist a good biscuit.'

Janette busied herself sorting everyone out before taking a seat across from Magda. Her garden was beautiful, Magda felt slightly envious. Her own, although spacious, was showing signs of recent neglect. Still, she reassured herself, she had plenty of time to do it now she was no longer working.

Janette went on to tell her that she worked as a social worker.

'Really? I'm a counsellor, or at least I was. I'm hoping to have some time out, but then look for another job.'

'Well I work for a local health trust. We're always desperate for good counsellors. Just give me the nod and I'll find out what's available. Happy to put in a good word for you too. I can tell already you're the type of person we'd love on our team.'

Magda found tears in her eyes suddenly at such an endorsement. 'That's really kind, thank you. You don't know me though.'

'I know a good one instinctively when I meet them and you're most definitely one of those.' Without a word she handed Magda a napkin with which to wipe her eyes.

'This is why I need some time out. The least little thing starts me going.' Magda blotted the tears as she busied herself giving a biscuit to each of the dogs.

'Yes, bereavement is so hard. People don't know what to say and so they say nothing, or keep their distance. It's such an English thing.' Magda nodded agreement and was taken right back, in that instance to the graveside and how Margaret and Roisin had wailed all through the burial.

Janette was right, this stiff upper lip, say nothing attitude was indeed very English.

'Now let me tell you some more about Max' Magda was grateful for Janette's quick change of subject. 'He's the loveliest of men, but a dreadful flirt. You'll need to be on guard as he'll swallow someone as beautiful as you, whole. He's a lecturer at Cambridge, very clever, but not at all opinionated which gives him a lot of charm. He's been divorced twice, and my guess would be for serial womanising! You'll like him though, he's a lot of fun. The Griffiths as I say, when they grace us with their presence are quite different. He is an awful womaniser, but not in the way Max is. With Ray it's something more invidious. You will really need to be on your guard against him. Poor Emily, that's his wife, has a terrible time of things. Why she doesn't leave him I will never know and don't get me started on the children. Two more spoilt brats I have yet to meet. I tell you what, why don't I give a dinner party the next time they're down? That way you can meet us all. It'll just be some home cooking, some pretty decent wine and a *get to know your neighbours* kind of thing. Nothing formal or intimidating. What do you say?'

There was something about Janette that reminded Magda of Beth. It was the same good heartedness. She found herself agreeing and even wondered if that might not be a good weekend to ask her former neighbour to come down. Kind of *the old neighbour meeting the new* so to speak.

'They'll be here about mid- month I expect. They come every two to three weeks in the summer and you just missed them. I'll give Emily a ring and then we can take it from there. Now look I'm off work this week so if you need anything, anything at all then do please give me a shout. As I say we're a friendly little lot, the Griffiths' odious children notwithstanding.' Magda found herself warming more and more towards her new neighbour and by the time she took her leave, felt that she had actually made a new friend.

Janette insisted on cutting a bunch of flowers for Magda to take back to the cottage. 'Brighten the place up a bit. Things like flowers make a new house a home.'

Magda thanked her and calling the two dogs, who had curled up in a heap under a shady tree, she went back home.

Chapter Three

THAT afternoon the television engineer arrived to install the satellite dish. Not a great television watcher, she still felt it would be good company and also wanted the phone and broadband package on offer. The engineer was cheerful and efficient. He also liked the dogs and recognised their breed, which endeared him to her from the off. He accepted a cup of tea, but carried on working explaining that this was his last call and he wanted to get home to his own dog, a rescued Greyhound.

If all the people are like him and Janette then it's going to be so lovely living here Magda thought remembering the isolation of London, particularly after Dennis had gone. When the engineer had finished, she raided the small store of food she had brought with her, noting that the following day she would need to do a big shop. She made a meal and sat eating outside as the evening was warm. She loved the way the darkness encroached, wrapping her in its velvety smoothness. There wasn't a sound apart from the occasional overhead plane and then, as the evening turned into night, the cry of a nocturnal animal and bird.

Looking at her watch, she found it was almost ten-thirty and so she made her way back inside. She put the dirty crockery into the dishwasher and made herself a cup of tea. Today had been a lazy one, so tomorrow would need to be busy she thought as she took the tea and her current novel upstairs to bed. The dogs had made their way up earlier and were firmly ensconced under the light summer duvet. The lamplight made the room warm and inviting. The walls were a pale apricot and despite having wanted to paint them her favourite lilac Magda decided she liked the warm feeling the colour generated and that she would leave it as it was. *I'll have to buy curtains though*, she thought. *A nice deep cream maybe*. She snuggled down and opened her book. After a few lines she found her eyes closing. She made a valiant effort to stay awake, but abandoning her tea, made her way into the little en-suite to clean her teeth before settling back into bed and into a deep sleep.

Her dreams, when they came, however, were less than peaceful. She was in her garden, but not safe, she knew. There was a menace from somewhere, of that she was aware. She could hear shouts, calling, calling, rough voices that she knew meant her harm. She ran and ran. Reaching the gate, she fumbled with the lock and couldn't get it to open. She was in grave danger; that much she knew also. Rushing back inside she found the cottage was changed, not at all how it was in reality. It was old, dingy with drab walls and carpet. The windows were small and dirty not letting in much light.

The shouting was getting nearer, and there was a banging on the door. She had to get away, she had to and then – nothing.

Gradually she became aware of her surroundings as she woke. The banging though continued. Groggily, she sat up, realising that in fact there was someone banging at her door. Shrugging on her dressing gown she went downstairs.

'Hello love, British Gas – Meter Reading?' The man on the step was very real. She hadn't realised that she needed to read her meter. In fact, she didn't even know where it was.

'Sorry, have you been here before?' She asked, hoping that he might enlighten her as to the meter's whereabouts.

'Nah, not me. Shall I come in and have a scout round?' He pulled a laminated badge bearing his likeness, hung on a lanyard, forward for her inspection.

'If you don't mind?' Magda turned and walked in with him following closely behind. The dogs, alerted by the arrival of a stranger started to bark.

'Hang on, I'll just let the dogs out.' Magda felt wrong-footed. She had been woken from something sinister so quickly it was hard to separate reality from fiction.

'Here you go love, in this cupboard, in your utility.' The gas man revealed two very new looking meters. 'All good, all British Safety Standard. New see. That's why we needed to have a look. I've taken the readings for you.' He shook hands as she led him back outside.

Wearily she trudged back in and put on the kettle. She fed the dogs, made coffee and sat down on the kitchen bench. Wisps of the dream kept floating back to her. The shouting, the feeling of menace, the not being able to escape. It had all seemed so vivid, so real. Mentally she shook herself. It was just a dream she told herself, nothing real, a dream. It's because, despite how at home you feel, it's still a new place. It needs some getting used to.

She busied around getting breakfast, having a shower and then decided she was going to the nearest town to do a big shop. Ramsey was small, so she thought, looking online that she might try Peterborough. She needed food, curtains for the bedroom, paint, household bits and pieces. She was sure she would find everything there. It was too warm to take the dogs though and leave them in the car. This was a dilemma. Then she remembered Janette and her offer of help. Searching for the spare key, she set off down the path to Janette's cottage.

Janette was happy to come in she said and to let them out around lunchtime.

'Do you want me to take them for a walk? I can do that. I won't let them off the lead or anything.'

'Really? You wouldn't mind? That would be amazing.'

'No problem. The exercise will do me good. Leave their leads somewhere accessible and I'll take them this afternoon.'

'Oh Janette, you're a star, thank you so much. See you later.' And with that Magda went back in and settled the dogs, leaving their leads on the kitchen table. She gathered her bags and a list she had made earlier, and locking up, got into her car and drove off.

The journey was a bit longer than she had thought and she thanked God for the newly installed satnav. She would never have found her way along the winding lanes without it. She drove alongside ditches or dykes as she knew they were called round here, trying not to get distracted by the wonderful views either side of the road. Finally, she found a sign saying she had entered Peterborough. The satnav duly told her where she might park, eschewing a huge multi storey car park for an one open to the skies almost right in the centre. She bought a ticket from the machine, gathered her bags and wandered into the city.

It was a nice city, large but not overwhelming. The Cathedral dominated the skyline and in the square before it there were pigeons, a burger van and plenty of shops. No food shops though. She wondered where they might be. She bought all she needed, even going into a large *Waterstones* where she stocked up on books. She had no idea if there was a library local to her and needed to make sure she had plenty to read. Finally, she discovered an ASDA store and was able to stock up on food after she had taken advantage of its cafeteria and had a sandwich and a cup of tea.

The journey home seemed even longer as she was so tired. Every now and then pictures from the dream would flash into her mind. Determined not to let them bother her, she put a disc into the CD player and listened to Coldplay as she drove. The songs reminded her of Dennis, but in a good way, which she took to mean she might be healing a little.

When she got home, she parked in her driveway and began to unload the car.

'Hello there. Say, do you need a hand?'

The voice was coming from a smiling man as Magda turned. He was quite tall, slim with reddish blonde slightly receding hair and a well-trimmed beard.

'I'm Max by the way, from next door, not a psychopathic stalker.'

Magda liked his smile and realised in an instant why Janette had said he was attractive. Not good looking in a conventional sense, but he had a mobile face with a cheerful, kind expression. His blue eyes twinkled at her as he made to take two of the bags from her outstretched hands.

'Here let me. You go on and open the door and I'll help unload this lot.'

With great determination he removed two more carrier bags from the boot and strode purposefully up the path. Magda, having located the keys in her capacious, sack-like leather handbag, opened the door for him. He insisted on carrying in all the bags.

'Thank you that's so kind. I'm Magda.'

Max shook her hand. 'Hello Magda and welcome to the neighbourhood as they say.' He was indeed charming.

'Can I offer you a cup of tea or anything?'

'Oh, my goodness, look at you two, how delightful. Hello there boys or is it girls? Oh boys I see. Come and say Hello to Uncle Max.' Max had spotted the two dogs who had come out to inspect what was going on and more importantly to find out what was in the many shopping bags, ever hopeful for a treat or two.

'Oh yes, boys. Aymes and Rollins, come and meet Max.'

'Cricket fan?' Max looked up from where he was bending, fussing the dogs, a questioning gleam in his bright eyes.

'My husband was…my late husband that is.'

'Late in the sense of…? Oh, my goodness, so sorry, you really do mean late don't you? It's just that I associate widows with being a bit old and wrinkly, not beautiful young ladies like you. Sorry again, that sounds very crass, doesn't it?'

Despite herself, Magda found herself laughing. He was irrepressible that was for sure.

'Forgive me, I really didn't mean to offend you. Gosh, that's the last thing. I am very, very happy to have a neighbour, and a beautiful one too if you don't mind my saying? Mrs G was lovely but rather elderly when I arrived and very, very forgetful. I did my best to help the poor old girl, but being rung at three in the morning to ask why *Casualty* wasn't on the television was a bit above and beyond the call of duty! I had to contact her son, who was not best pleased as he lives in Australia. She went into a care home poor old thing. I visited her sometimes. The cottage stayed empty though. It wasn't done up till she died.'

Once again she read the kindness and compassion in what he was saying. Okay so he was a flirt, that was obvious, but he also had a kind heart, which mattered most.

'Well I too am happy to be here. Thanks for your help with the bags. Would you like something to drink?'

'Normally I would accept with alacrity, but alas I was just on my way out. How about tomorrow evening, if that's not being too forward?'

Laughingly she shook her head. 'Tomorrow would be fine. It's the least I can do now I know I've held you up.'

'Not at all dear lady. I will see you, and these delightful little cricketers at say – seven thirty tomorrow evening?'

'Yes, that would be lovely. Do you mind if I invite Janette? She was lovely and she came in to let the dogs out today whilst I was out.'

'Ah Janette and I are the best of friends. Well, we all have to stick together out here in the sticks. If the power goes off or our phones go down, we have to be here for our neighbours. Mind you, you'll be alright in the event of a power cut as I know Dan, Mrs G's son, put a generator in that old shed at the back. Have you found it yet?'

Magda shook her head. She hadn't even spotted an old shed.

'No, I haven't.'

Well it's a bit hidden by a trellis and some wall. Do you want me to show you?'

'Oh no, I've held you up enough. Maybe another time. Anyway, I would have absolutely no idea how to get a generator to work or what it needs to fuel it.'

Max smiled and raised an eyebrow.

'I never disappoint a damsel in distress. Tomorrow when I come round, I'll give you your first lesson in generator management. And before you say anything, you can repay me by allowing me to shelter in case of a power cut.'

Magda smiled and agreed as she ushered him out.

Exhausted, she fed the dogs then opened one of the ready meals she had bought and put it in the microwave. Proper cooking tomorrow she vowed as she put things away in cupboards, fridge and freezer. She had been gratified to see that the freezer in the utility room was of the chest variety and capacious. That would mean less shopping trips. She knew that along the road there was a garage with a Tesco express but hadn't managed to locate it yet. Other than that there were little in the way of amenities.

The microwave pinged to let her know that the meal was ready, and after pouring herself a glass of wine, she took it out and ate it straight from the container.

Later that evening, when she felt a bit more human, she telephoned Beth to give her the phone number. They chatted for about half an hour. Beth laughed about Max and said how glad she was about Janette and that it sounded as if Magda would not be lonely. She said she had seen no sign of the Axelrods yet. She ended by saying she missed Magda and *her boys* and that she looked forward to keeping in touch. Magda reassured her that this would happen no matter what, before they disconnected.

In Peterborough Magda had bought some lovely curtains, the colour of clotted cream and she wanted to put them up before going to bed. Luckily there was a wooden curtain pole already in situ so all she would need to do was add the hooks she had bought and then attach these to the pole. Not too onerous, she laughed to herself as she embarked on the task.

She had some trouble locating the smaller of her two step ladders but found it behind the door in the utility room. Grabbing it, she took it and the curtains upstairs and began to hang them. The bedroom looked out over the garden at the back and just as she hung the last hook, she noticed a flash of white that seemed to race across the lawn and then disappear. She waited to see if it returned and wondered what or whom it might be. It looked too big for a barn owl and anyway it was at ground level. *Not a fox - wrong colour*. She waited another few minutes before giving up. Must have been a trick of the light, she thought as she folded the ladder and drew the curtains across the window. She was gratified to see that they fit perfectly. She had never been good with measuring things. That had always been Dennis' domain. The thought made her sad.

'Come on boys, last trip outside for you.'

Determinedly, she made herself cheerful as she ushered the two dogs out into the garden. Aymes, the more nervous of the two seemed to have other ideas. Instead of racing out to join his brother, now happily watering a lilac bush, he cowered behind Magda and it took a lot of coaxing for her to get him out.

'What's the matter little boy? Didn't you like Auntie Janette taking you out?' Despite her resolution never to be one of those who talked to their pets as they would people, she had quickly succumbed to the habit. At last, with a look at her, which seemed to say *How could you?* Aymes rushed outside, quickly relieved himself on the same bush and ran back in as if the hounds of hell were after him. He refused his little milky biscuit that Magda gave them last thing at night before finally agreeing to take it from her outstretched hand. Ruffling his head, she turned and made her way upstairs to bed. She cleaned her teeth, got undressed and snuggled under the summer duvet. A shiver passed over her, despite the heat and she realised suddenly that only Rollins was snuggled on the bed.

'Where's that silly brother of yours got to?'

She heaved herself up and out of bed. A quick search of the room finally revealed him hiding underneath the bed and shivering.

'Come on boy. This isn't like you. I promise I won't leave you to Auntie Janette tomorrow.'

It took a bit of coaxing but finally he emerged and went, not on top but right down into the bed under the duvet. *Funny little dog* was Magda's last thought as she drifted into sleep.

Chapter Four

THE evening with Max and Janette went off very well. Instead of just being a few drinks it turned into dinner with Max ordering a takeaway.

'It'll probably be cold by the time it gets here, eh Janette? But we can soon heat it up.' He continued to turn on the charm, despite Janette's various snorts and eye rolling! Magda didn't mind as felt continuously just as she had yesterday, that his heart was in the right place. When she asked if he was married he snorted and told her 'Twice bitten, twice shy.' With a laugh. 'But you never know, I could still be open to offers.'

The two women felt relaxed enough by then to laugh openly and despite his pretence of being hurt Max soon joined in. The meal when it arrived and was duly heated up was delicious. It was from an Indian restaurant in Ramsey and before she knew what was happening, Magda found herself having agreed to visit it one evening with Janette and Max. *There's certainly no question of being isolated* she thought as she cleared the plates into the kitchen. Beth was going to be very pleased.

The next morning was as hot as the previous one. As before Magda let the dogs out, fed them and then after preparing her breakfast took it out to the table under the pergola. Aymes and Rollins were playing with a ball they had unearthed from their toy box earlier. There wasn't a cloud in the sky, nor a sound to be heard apart from that of birdsong. This is truly heavenly, Magda thought. Now if I could find a way of getting a newspaper - she was addicted to cryptic crosswords - everything would be perfect. Rousing herself she decided to take the dogs and walk to the garage in search of one.

After a few twists and turns she managed to find the garage with the Tesco Extra next door. There was a rack of newspapers outside. Magda chose one and tying the dogs to a handy railing went in to buy it.

On the way home she walked by the river. She wondered to herself as she walked, why she felt so at home in this part of the world. She was a Londoner born and bred. But there was something about this place with its river, dykes and wide-open spaces that seemed to call to her soul. She felt as if she had lived here forever and that London had been another life. The dogs frolicked in and out of the dykes and came out shaking the drops of water all over her. The day was exceedingly hot and becoming heavy and airless, so Magda was quite glad of the cool, if rather muddy, shower.

After a while she decided to walk home so calling to the dogs she turned back.

The day seemed to get hotter and hotter. It felt like an oven. Once home Magda fed the dogs, made herself a sandwich and a cup of tea and took both out to sit under the pergola in the garden.

After she had eaten, she found her eyes closing as sleep began to claim her. She was just drifting off when she heard voices coming from what sounded like the end of the garden. Wide awake now, she looked over but could see no one there. It had sounded a childlike voice, speaking a foreign language – there it was again.

'Aspetta, aspetta, vieni qua.'

Magda got up and walked over but still she could see no one. Puzzled she walked back to the bench and sat down. It must be some kind of echo, she thought, something about the horseshoe shape of how the houses are built. I expect they were in Janette's garden. She remembered that Janette had two grown up sons and a grown-up daughter and that she was due to become a grandmother any day now. She had told Magda how excited she was at the prospect. *Oh, that's lovely then, Janette's family must be visiting.* Looking round she could see that Rollins had curled up in one of the dog baskets that Magda had placed under a shady tree. There was no sign of Aymes. She walked inside and called him. She waited but the little dog didn't come.

'Where are you boy. Come on Aymes,' she shouted as she explored the downstairs rooms. They were empty so she walked upstairs, calling as she went. She found him hiding under the bed as he had been the night before. He was shivering and refused to be coaxed out.

Turning, she went downstairs to the fridge and found a piece of ham. Ham was something neither dogs could resist. She gave Rollins his piece and went back up to get Aymes from his hiding place. It took ages, much showing him the ham and calling until finally he deigned to emerge. Grudgingly he took the slice of ham and munched it steadily, occasionally looking under the bed as if there was something there he didn't like.

'You're a funny little dog,' she whispered to him as eventually he agreed to accompany her downstairs.

Later, just as she was finishing her dinner, there was a loud tap on the window. Going over she saw Max grinning broadly at her.

'Hello, we didn't get a chance last time for me to show you the workings of the generator. It looks as if it could be stormy later so I thought I'd come over and show you now.'

'Yes, I agree and it's so hot. Hang on I'll just get my shoes.'

Magda found her sandals, slipped them on and joined him outside on the lawn. She followed him down the garden and there, as he had said, was the low brick wall with the trellis, behind which sat a small wooden shed. Opening it Magda gasped as she spied a strange looking machine that squatted there like an alien from outer space.

Max, however, was thrilled with it. 'There you are I told you, and it's brand new too. Look it's filled with fuel as well.' He sounded so excited like a child receiving his best Christmas present. It made Magda laugh.

'Here, look all you do is fill this bit with this.' He indicated a can of petrol next to it. 'You don't need to at the moment as it's full. Then you pull this handle here and – voila!'

The machine cranked into life with a shudder and Magda took a step back in alarm. Max turned it off with another lever.

'There, easy!' He beamed. 'Now if the power goes out and it will mark my words if we do get that storm then all you need to do is grab a torch and head down here. Then you pull the lever as I showed you – easy.'

Magda racked her brains as to whether she even had a torch. In Highgate with all its street lighting and reliable source of electricity, a torch was not exactly an essential item. She hesitated not wanting Max to think she was a total idiot.

However, he must have picked up on it as he laughed. 'Don't tell me, you don't have a torch? Not to worry I've got two indoors and one in the car. I'll let you have one of mine. Keep it as long as you like, give it back when you've got yourself one.'

He walked off towards his house and came back bearing a huge rubberised torch. 'There you go, batteries and everything. You'll need one living out here.'

Thanking him, Magda asked if he would like to come in for a drink.

'Just a quick one, sadly. I've got a big day tomorrow, but yes please.'

They walked back inside and Magda opened a bottle of red wine and poured them each a glass. In the end they ended up drinking two glasses apiece before Max told her he really ought to be making a move. Magda found him very easy to talk to. He had a good sense of humour and didn't mind laughing at himself, something which put her in mind of Dennis who had had the same quality.

'I'll go out the back way, if that's alright? I can just hop over the fence then.'

Just as she showed him out, the storm broke and there was a gigantic clap of thunder.

'Told you. Never mind, you're safe and you've got the Genny.' With a final wave of the hand he leapt the fence like a hurdler and disappeared into his own garden.

Magda made herself a cup of tea and took it and her book up to bed. The dogs, obviously frightened by the storm had buried deep under the duvet. Magda undressed and settled down to read. However, this soon became impossible as the storm took hold and gigantic thunderclaps and sheets of forked lighting lit up the room.

Abandoning her book Magda went to clean her teeth and then settled into bed but sleep proved elusive. The storm raged and the lightning was visible even with the curtains closed. It was like a giant pyrotechnic display going on in her back garden. After about half an hour, she sat up and turned on the bedside light to try again to read. The light kept flickering and then going dim, but so far the electricity had stayed on.

She managed a chapter, but feeling her eyes closing, went to settle back down. Just then there was an enormous crack of thunder and it felt as if the house shook. *Don't be silly* Magda reassured herself, *you know from the deeds that this was built in the eighteenth century. It's stood that long, it's not going to collapse now*. Reasoning did nothing, so she decided to go downstairs for more tea. The dogs, unusually for them did not follow her.

She filled the kettle and switched it on. Outside in the garden everything was being flattened by the torrential rain. Magda bemoaned her poor shrubs as she watched the garden illuminated yet again by forks of lightning. Just as the kettle boiled, everything went dark. Fumbling the tea bag out of the mug, she put it in the sink. She wondered for a moment or two if she should go and start the generator. The thought of going even that short distance in this weather was less than appealing. She reasoned also that the food in the freezer would keep for at least twenty-four hours if she didn't open the lid. *The power's bound to be on by the morning* she thought wearily as she made her way back upstairs to bed and this time thankfully, fell into a deep sleep.

Chapter Five

AS she had predicted when she woke the clock on her bedside was flashing its green digits, indicating that the power had been restored. She groped for her watch, feeling groggy from such a poor night's sleep. She was amazed to find it had gone nine. The dogs hadn't even stirred which was unusual for them. She got out of bed and went downstairs. They rushed down after her and she let them into the garden.

The garden looked dreadful. As she had thought, the shrubs had been almost flattened. There was a branch hanging off the old tree in the corner. The petals of some of the flowers were strewn over the lawn. Despite such a massive storm however, the day was as hot as its predecessors. *So, it's a day working in the garden then*, Magda thought as she prepared the dogs' breakfast and then her own.

Walking outside she looked over the fence to see if Max was still there. She wanted to thank him again for his help the night before. His car had gone, so he had left for work. She decided to write him a little note and put it through his door later. She was very grateful to have found him and Janette and didn't want either of them to think she was a nuisance, lonely or incapable.

After breakfast and another walk with the dogs to the garage she started to tidy the ravaged garden. She found a few gardening tools in the shed and managed to lop the fallen branch. She wondered if Max or Janette had a wood burner and if they would like the log if they had. She moved it over to the edge of the garden and began to rake the fallen petals and to tidy back the shrubs.

A quiet cough behind her made her turn round and standing in her garden was a strange man. He was tall with fair hair that fell across his forehead. He had the most startling blue eyes she had ever seen. They were almost turquoise. He was dressed in old-fashioned trousers with turn ups and a long, belted raincoat despite the heat of the day.

'Excuse me.' His voice was low and cultured. 'But I thought this was Lavender Cottage. Do you know it? Lavender Cottage I mean.'

Magda hadn't seen a cottage with that name, but perhaps that was the one belonging to the Griffiths.

'I don't I'm afraid, but it could be the one second from the end.'

'No, no, I'm sure it's one of these two. Do you happen to know Maria by any chance?'

'I'm sorry I don't. I've only been here less than a week. There's a lady though on the end, Bramble Cottage. She's been here a while. She might know Maria.'

Thoughtfully the man gazed at her before turning abruptly and walking off, without even a *thank you*.

How strange, and rather rude, thought Magda as she turned back to the shrubs. I wonder who he is. There had been something very strange about him. She couldn't stop thinking about his compelling eyes. *Oh well, I expect Janette will know where he can find Maria,* she thought as she abandoned the pruning in favour of some lunch.

While she was eating, she wondered suddenly if Maria could be the name of one of Max's ex-wives. She vowed to ask Max next time they met, but on the other hand didn't want to offend him by asking about an ex. She hoped the stranger had found Janette in and had been able to ask her. Finishing her lunch, she resumed her gardening without giving another thought to the stranger.

A few days later Janette called to say that the Griffiths were arriving at the weekend and the dinner party would be Saturday evening. Max was coming and the Griffiths were looking forward to meeting Magda.

When Saturday arrived, she felt nervous. She had not been anywhere on her own since Dennis died. It felt strange as for so long she had been part of a couple. She took a lot of trouble choosing her outfit.

Eventually she decided on a long cotton skirt and a silk vest top. She washed and dried her hair, putting it up into a loose knot. She found a bottle of wine to go with the box of chocolates she had bought at the garage to take with her.

At seven thirty she presented herself at Janette's front door.

'Oh, lovely, Magda. Come on in. Thank you, you didn't have to.'

Janette took the proffered gifts and led Magda inside. This was the first time she had been inside Janette's cottage, having only had a glimpse en-route to the garden, the day they had coffee together. The lay out had more of a thirties feel to it than her own cottage. It was homely though and she sat down on a comfy chair.

'This is Ray and his wife, Emily. And this you two is Magda our new girl.' Janette laughed as she said this last bit before leaving them to fetch Magda a glass of wine from the kitchen.

Magda took an immediate dislike to Ray Griffiths who sat there leering at her, whilst trying to make conversation. It was clear that he was being patronising and Magda felt a wave of sympathy for Emily who seemed a very sweet woman. There was no sign of their children. Ignoring Ray, Magda asked their whereabouts but Emily gave a nervous glance at her husband before answering.

'Oh, they're at home watching a film. They didn't want to come tonight.'

'Didn't want to spend the evening with a bunch of old fogies.' Ray boomed, guffawing loudly, obviously pleased with himself. Just then the doorbell rang and Janette ushered in Max. Never before had Magda felt so relieved to see someone. She sent him a desperate signal with her eyes, which he must have picked up as he came and sat between herself and Ray.

'So, Max how's the world of academia eh? Sleepy as ever. I wonder what you lot would make of a week or two working in the city?'

Max, in his usual affable manner took no offence and answered Ray in the same jovial manner.

'Oh, we'd fold within a week, I'm sure.'

This provoked another loud guffaw from Ray as Magda surreptitiously glanced at her watch, wondering how long she would have to stay. Janette returned with some bits and pieces to snack on, saying that dinner would be at least another half an hour. *No early escape then* Magda thought as she took a handful of nuts from the proffered bowl.

Dinner when it was ready was delicious, but much to her dismay, Janette had put Ray next to her at the dining table. Janette sat on her other side, but she was up and down getting things and making sure everyone had what they needed. Emily Griffiths was so quiet Magda sometimes forgot she was there. She tried in vain to engage her in conversation, but the replies she gave were usually monosyllabic, leaving no room for further discussion. Magda noticed this also applied to Max when he tried to talk to Emily. Ray, however, held forth endlessly. Once Magda caught Max's eye and he smiled in a conspiratorial fashion, making her smile.

'Shall we take our coffee into the garden?' Janette asked when the meal was finally over. Nobody demurred and so they walked out to sit where Magda had the first time she visited Janette. This jogged her memory and as they sat down, she asked Janette about the mysterious man who had been trying to find Maria.

'No, he didn't come here. When was it did you say?'

'The day after the storm.'

'No, definitely not and I was in all that day too. Sorry.' Magda smiled.

'Oh, it doesn't matter. It was just that he was so certain he had the right place and that Maria lived where I do, although he thought the cottage was called *Lavender Cottage* not Hornbeams.'

'Very strange. But I love a mystery. Let me know if he calls again, won't you?'

Magda turned to Max. 'Sorry Max, I don't mean to be rude or anything, but is one of your exes called Maria?'

Max laughed. 'That's not being rude and no my dear, no Maria amongst them. Melissa and Delia were my two as you put it exes.' His warm smile reassured her that he had not been offended.

Both she and Max tried to wait it out until the Griffiths left. Magda wanted to tell Janette just how much she disliked Ray.

Finally, at around eleven they stood up.

'Got to be on our way, I'm afraid. The wife needs her beauty sleep.' He cast what could only be a disparaging look in Emily's direction.

Janette ushered them out, mouthing, 'Stay there' to Magda and Max.

She soon returned with a bottle of brandy. 'Well what did you think?' She directed her question at Magda.

'I thought Ray was one of the most obnoxious people I have ever met.'

'There you go, I told you and you agree don't you Max?'

'I do indeed. There's been many a time I'd have liked to knock his block off. Dreadful man and his poor long-suffering wife. You wait till you meet the children. Talk about spoilt brats!'

Magda smiled. They finished off the night with a glass of brandy each before making their way home.

'Thank you, Janette. The meal was lovely. You and Max must come over and let me cook for you one evening. I won't be inviting the Griffiths though I'm afraid, unless I could persuade Emily on her own.'

'You've as much chance of that as the proverbial snowball in hell.' Max said, taking her arm to guide her along the dark road back home. At the door he kissed her on both cheeks, continental style, before leaving her at her front door. As before he went into the garden and hopped over the fence to his own property with a cheery wave.

Magda let herself in and was greeted ecstatically by an excited Rollins.

'Where's your brother then?' Magda asked as she stroked his head. Looking in the dog basket there was once again no sign of him. This time she didn't hesitate. She ran up the stairs and bending to look under her bed, she found him there, curled up and disturbingly he was shivering again, despite the intense heat. This time he did emerge more willingly and with a little coaxing condescended to come down with her. However, when she opened the back door he refused to go out, despite Rollins bounding out in front. He would only agree to go when Magda herself walked into the garden. *He's a funny little dog*, she thought. *I wonder if he's missing Beth.* They had both spent a lot of time with the former neighbour.

As soon as he had relieved himself on the nearest bush, Aymes, once again, raced back in as if the hounds of hell were after him. At first he refused the milky bone biscuit, only relenting a few minutes later. *I'll need to keep an eye on him*, Magda thought, although he was eating alright which she felt he wouldn't do if he was that unhappy, or worse, ill.

When she got to bed, she found it hard to sleep. She turned on her bedside light and read for a while. Only when she felt her eyelids becoming heavy did she lay down. And that night she had vivid and disturbing dreams.

There were planes flying overhead and they were sinister, she recognised that much. There was danger and it was coming from down on the ground, but she was afraid also for someone flying up in the air. The next thing she knew she was running, running down the garden, out of the gate and onto the road, the planes still overhead. She shouted, 'Stay safe, stay safe,' before waking, shaking and sweating, her heart thumping wildly although she was safely in her own bed.

She lay there panting and exhausted. It took her a while to reconnect with reality. The dream had been so real, so vivid and so frightening. There had been such an air of menace to it. She had felt the danger both from down on the ground and in the sky.

Once again only Rollins was in evidence and she guessed that Aymes had gone back under the bed. *Oh God I hope this house isn't haunted!* Suddenly she remembered someone at her old work talking about one of their cats not liking the new house. Somebody else had suggested that the house could be haunted and the cat was sensing it. *No of course it can't be* she admonished herself. *It feels lovely and peaceful and an old lady lived here and probably died peacefully here too.* She knew she was being fanciful, but the dream had scared her so much.

Looking at the bedside clock, she saw it was only twenty past three. She didn't feel at all tired and got up and went to make herself yet another cup of tea. Taking it back to bed, she tried to read, but images from the dream kept intruding, making concentration impossible. As she lay down again, she admitted to herself that she was slightly reluctant to return to sleep in case the dream came again. More than anything she wished she had Dennis next to her, to reassure her as he had done so many times during their eight-year marriage.

Something else, something, unacknowledged surfaced. Dennis had wanted a baby after five years of marriage, but she had refused, saying she wasn't ready for a family. She had worked hard to reach her standing at work and didn't want to jeopardise that. Now she realised how selfish she had been, to deny Dennis and how welcome another presence in her life connected with her husband would be. Finally, she felt herself drifting off.

Luckily there were no more dreams. When she woke, she felt refreshed and ready for the new day. Both dogs were tangled together, sleeping in a heap, the sun was shining and the birds were singing and all this helped to banish the dark happenings of the previous night.

Magda got up went downstairs, let the dogs out, had breakfast and then decided she was, at last, going to sort out her books in the study. She walked in and thought how stuffy it felt. She opened the little window, but the day was airless again, with no breeze. She placed the empty bookshelves where she wanted them and was thrilled to notice that there were also some built in ones, that looked new, in the small alcove. She felt again a gratitude to the previous owner and her son or grandson - she couldn't remember now whom the agent had told her had inherited the cottage. Whoever it was they had done a wonderful renovation. It almost felt as if they had known she was coming.

She worked hard, stopping only for a mid- morning cup of tea before returning to the task. She took a quick lunch break and fed the dogs. At around four thirty she had every box unpacked and every book placed onto a shelf. They were also in some kind of order, something she had not achieved before despite having always been a bibliophile with a huge collection since childhood.

A cheery voice hailed her and when she went outside she found Max standing in the garden with a bottle of wine.

'This is a bribe I'm afraid,' he announced cheerfully as he handed it over. 'I've got to go away for a few days: conference in Amsterdam and I was wondering if you'd mind keeping an eye on things for me and popping in to water the plants?'

'Of course I will. I owe you anyway for the generator lesson.'

Max laughed. 'Did you use it the other night, when the power went out?'

'Well no, but I would have done if it had still been off the next morning. I couldn't face the walk down the garden in all that thunder, lightning and rain.'

'What a girly girl!'

Magda pretended to swipe at him.

'Never mind, we'll toughen you up, Janette and I - get you used to life in the country.'

'If I open this, will you join me for a glass?'

'Yes, please. I thought you'd never ask.'

Magda was beginning to like him more and more.

They settled in the garden with their wine and Max produced his spare door key. 'I've still got a few plants, left from the former Mrs Matthews. She took off in a hurry and forgot them. Only joking, she actually left them for me, but only because she thought I'd kill them with neglect. I've bloody well-tended the buggers for a year, just to show her and I'd hate them to die now. It's so hot at the moment, they need almost constant water.'

Magda laughed. 'I must get some indoor plants for my house. I only had a couple and they were so tall I thought they'd be up to the ceiling in the cottage, so I left them with my lovely neighbour.' At this Magda found her eyes filling with tears. Surreptitiously she tried to wipe them before Max saw.

'Hey, what is it?'

She had been found out. 'It's nothing, just being silly. It's just that Beth, my neighbour was so sweet and helpful when Dennis had his accident. I honestly don't know how I would have got through it without her. She was the one who made me adopt the dogs. I guess I miss her, that's all. Oh, and I had a really horrid dream last night, that scared me so I feel a bit wobbly today.'

Max leant across the table and took her hand. 'So sorry. Sounds as if you've had quite a year. It must have been dreadful to lose your husband in the way you did. Then moving here. That was brave. I'm sure your lovely neighbour misses you too, but you'll go and visit won't you? London's not that far.'

Magda sniffed. 'I know, as I say, just being wobbly and silly. It's been lovely moving here. You and Janette have been brilliant and I was wanting to see you to talk about how awful the Griffiths are. I know we said a bit briefly but my god that man!'

Max roared with laughter. 'So, you were not impressed by the pompous Mr Ray Griffiths then?'

'Not in the least!'

This made Max laugh even harder. 'That won't matter to him in the slightest; he's impressed enough with himself.'

They laughed a little longer together before Max turned the conversation back to something Magda had said earlier. 'Tell me about the dream that made you so upset?'

'Oh, I don't know. I expect it was nothing really. There were these planes up in the sky, I could hear them. Somehow I knew I was in danger and I was running away, but there was danger down on the ground too. It's just that it was so vivid, so real. It kind of spooked me.'

'Perhaps you were getting vibes from the airfield that used to be here in the war?' I'll find something about it for you to read. Planes took off to go and bomb Germany. I sometimes wonder if things leave, you know, an imprint or something. You're a therapist, haven't you read your Jung? The collective memory and all that?'

It made perfect sense to Magda when he said it. 'Gosh yes, of course I have, and you're right. This place is old so there must be a lot of distant memories within its walls. I never thought of that. Thank you, you've made me feel better already.'

Magda would not have said it or even acknowledged it to herself but all day, even as she was keeping busy, there had been a little bit of her that had been dreading going to sleep, just in case the dream came back. It was that awful sense of danger that had almost undone her.

A little later Max said he had to be going as he needed to pack so Magda wished him a good trip.

'I'll be back Thursday, but late, very late. My plane doesn't get in until 11.30pm and there's the drive from Birmingham. I'm leaving my car at the airport. I'll bring you back a stick of rock or a bunch of tulips, shall I? Or indeed anything from that city which might tempt you?' With raised eyebrows he mimed rolling a joint and sucking on it.

Magda smiled at this as she walked with him across the garden. As was his habit now, he leapt the fence and once again with a cheery wave, disappeared.

That night was dream free and Magda woke refreshed and ready for the day. She and the dogs had their usual walk to the garage for the paper. This time the lady inside greeted her like an old friend and asked where she lived. She told her and the lady came out with a bowl of water for the dogs.

'We've got a boy who delivers papers. Would you like us to add you to his route?'

'Oh, that would be good, although it gives me a good reason to come out and walk, but yes, please if he could. I can walk later then.'

Agreeing that this would begin the following morning, Magda thanked the lady, who said her name was Linda, and untying the dogs, she waved goodbye and set off down to the river.

As she was walking a plane flew overhead and for a second she was reminded of her dream. She felt calm though after her talk with Max.

It was another hot lazy day and in the afternoon Magda thought about how she might like to look for work. She had promised herself a year or two off, but the reality was that she was missing doing her job. She looked online but nothing within the vicinity took her fancy. She remembered Janette saying she would look out for something for her and made a mental to note to have a chat about it when they next met.

Janette had gone to Nottingham as the grandchild's birth was imminent and so, with Max gone too, Magda was in the little row of cottages on her own, the Griffiths having left the morning after the dinner party. As evening came Magda began to feel just a little anxious that she was there alone. She made herself some pasta and after she had eaten it, rang Beth.

Beth as always, was delighted to hear from her. She told her she had met Jeannie Axelrod, and quite liked her, but not nearly as much as she liked Magda. 'She's a little brash, but I think that's because she's American.'

Magda was sure that only the husband was American but she didn't say anything. It quite gladdened her heart to hear that the erstwhile Mrs Axelrod had not matched up to her in Beth's eyes.

Beth, of course wanted to know how the dogs were and Magda found herself telling her that Aymes seemed frightened at times.

'Oh dear, do you think you have a ghost?' Beth astounded her by asking.

'What do you mean?'

'Well animals are notoriously sensitive to things like that. You said the cottage was old and there could be a spirit there. I'm sure it won't do anyone any harm, but poor little Aymes is probably worried by it at the moment. He'll settle down when he realises it's benign.'

Suddenly Magda wished she hadn't said anything to Beth as now she was feeling quite frightened herself. *No*, she thought, *Max's explanation is far more likely.*

She and Beth chatted for another half an hour or so before Beth said she was going to have a nightcap, which Magda knew meant a glass of whisky, and then get off to bed.

'When are you coming to see me?' Beth said as they were ending their conversation. 'It would be lovely to see you and we could take the dogs into the woods.' Magda too felt that it would be nice to meet up so they arranged a Friday two weeks later as Beth said an old friend was visiting the following week.

The thought of going to see Beth cheered up Magda no end. Determined not to let talk of spirits and ghosts frighten her, she let the dogs into the garden and made a cup of tea to take up to bed. This time she put on the small television she had moved from the study into the bedroom and settled down to watch a murder mystery.

Every night for the next few nights she had the dream. It varied from time to time but the content was basically the same. She was in danger, running along the road towards the river and the planes were flying overhead. Sometimes voices were calling out behind her; Harsh, menacing voices she thought were male. There were lights blazing from the planes as they flew in some kind of formation. Although she was worried for herself, the danger for someone else was uppermost in her mind. Strangely she was barefoot and could feel the stones from the lane digging into her feet. She held a loose white garment, like something old-fashioned, around her and shivered in the bitter cold. Sometimes when she woke, heart pounding, head aching, sweating and afraid, she would look at the soles of her feet almost expecting them to be bleeding from the stones. They never were.

She began also to feel discomforted during the day. She missed Max and Janette and wished they would return. She almost thought the Griffiths would be welcome as some company in the deserted close.

On the day of Max's return, she was working in the garden when, halfway through the afternoon, she heard the gate open and close and a person behind her, clearing his throat. She turned and there was the man from before, the man who had been looking for Maria.

'Hello again.' He smiled at her.

This time instead of the raincoat, he was wearing a military uniform, blue grey with a brooch depicting outstretched wings. *He must be from one of the airbases*, she thought. She remembered there was one at Wittering, but didn't really know quite where that was.

'Hello. Can I help you? I asked my neighbours about Maria but they didn't know anyone of that name. I had a thought though, that she might be the lady who owned this cottage - the one who died?'

'Maria died?' There was such sadness as he said this, it made Magda's heart go out to him.

'Yes, I believe so. Her grandson, I think it was, inherited the cottage, I bought it from him.'

'No, no that can't be right. Maria doesn't have any children.' He indicated the wooden sign on the wall of the house. 'And this is called Hornbeams, Maria lives in Lavender Cottage. I remember that for sure.'

Magda didn't know what else to say. Without moving he simply stood there watching her. She began to feel scared. *Suppose he's some kind of psychopath. Max and Janette aren't here, I'm all alone, completely at his mercy.* However, as she looked into his eyes, although she saw sadness, there was nothing threatening about him at all.

'I'm so sorry, I really wish I could help you, but none of us seem to know Maria. There's a lady, Linda at the garage. She's been here a while. She may know where Maria is now.'

Suddenly, despite the heat Magda shivered. There was something so intense about this man. She recognised too that he was extremely good looking in a very patrician kind of way. Tall, slim with fair hair, now swept back off his forehead. His turquoise blue eyes seemed to bore into her as if he was looking right into her soul. A chiselled face with a straight nose and finely arched eyebrows, but it was his mouth that held her, captivated her. It was full and sensuous in such a masculine face.

'Oh, I do beg your pardon. Adrian Taylor-Beaumont.' He held out his hand for her to shake.

Wiping hers surreptitiously on her skirt she took his and was surprised at how icily cold it felt in her own warm fingers.

'Magda McClean' she told him. 'Can I offer you a cup of tea or anything?' He shook his head.

'I have to be going.' That was all he said abruptly turning to walk out through the garden gate.

Magda was unsure in which direction he went but could not get him out of her mind. She finished in the garden, had a shower and made herself a meal, which she took outside to eat. She wondered idly when or if the weather was going to break. Apart from that huge storm it had been hot and sunny ever since she arrived. *Next they'll be talking about water shortages and hose pipe bans*, she laughed to herself as she washed her dinner things in the sink.

She decided that the following day she would go shopping again. The supplies she had bought were diminishing and she had read three of the four books she got at the same time. She went into Max's house to water his plants and then got the hosepipe from her own garden and watered the outside plants for good measure as they were beginning to wilt.

Max's cottage was very like her own. She would be pleased to have his cheerful presence there again.

There were no bad dreams that night. Magda woke and felt much better but found her mind wandering back to the strange encounter in the garden. Again, she wondered who Maria was. Despite having her paper delivered every morning, she thought she might walk to the garage and ask Linda.

Then she remembered about going shopping. She needed things badly so would have to prioritise that.

She fed the dogs, made breakfast, which again she ate outside. She made sure both their water bowls were filled with fresh water, gave them some chews and treats and grabbing her handbag and carrier bags went out to the car.

On the doorstep she found a bowl of tulip bulbs and a stick of rock.

Aaah Max! She laughed to herself as she got in the car and headed over to Peterborough.

All the way there she kept thinking of her mystery man. There had been something so vulnerable about him. The counsellor in her wanted to help him at least to find Maria and she had an idea. If he came again, she would ask what Maria's surname was so they could look for her on the internet. That was probably even better than asking Linda, although it wouldn't hurt to do both. She told herself it was nothing to do with how attractive he was, he was just someone in need of help.

She managed to find a large Tesco store just on the edge of the city and bought a lot of food, so much that apart from bread milk and eggs, things like that, she would be able to last a month. Fruit, something she loved was a bit of a problem as it wouldn't keep, but she had seen some in the garage and would just have to make do with that.

She bought more books in *Waterstones* and came home. When she got in, she put everything away and then taking the dogs' leads from the hook clipped them on and set off for the garage.

Linda looked surprised to see her, then a bit cross. 'Didn't he deliver today? Honestly that boy! It's just so hard to get anyone, that's the only reason I keep him on. You know what it's like these days, parents don't think paper rounds are safe.'

Magda reassured her that the paper had been delivered safely and on time. 'No, the reason I'm here is that there's this man. He's called at my house a couple of times looking for someone called Maria. He seemed to think that she lived where I do now. The thing is he called my house Lavender Cottage. I know you've been here for a while; do you remember or know of a Maria round here?'

Linda thought for a moment or two. 'No not really, but I bet my mother in law would know. We usually go up and visit her every couple of weeks. Poor old thing's in a home now in Ely. She was born and grew up here. If anyone would know it would be her. There's nothing wrong with her mentally but she's severely disabled with arthritis and what with the shop and everything, Jim and I got so that we couldn't manage. Jim feels bad so we visit as often as possible.'

'Oh, that would be good, if you don't mind. He seems worried and looks so sad. I think he's from one of the airbases here as last time he was wearing his uniform.'

'Oh, Love there ain't no airbases here now. Nearest would be Wittering. Long way for him to come. There was one near here during the war, but that went years ago. Anyway, happen he might be on leave or something. Poor sod could be back from Afghanistan. Dreadful war that.'

Magda agreed, bought some apples and nectarines and thanked Linda again.

'Not a problem love and as I say, soon as me and Jim visit Margaret, I'll ask about your man and his Maria.'

Magda walked home slowly along the riverbank. It was still hot with hardly a cloud in the sky. It was July now. She realised with a start she'd been here over a month. She wondered whether Janette's granddaughter had been born yet. She knew the baby was a girl and was going to be called Rose. She wished she'd asked Janette for her mobile number so she could have rung her to find out. *Never mind*, she thought, *at least Max is home again. I won't feel as isolated tonight.* When she got in, she fed the dogs and made herself a mushroom omelette. She made a salad to go with it and took it out into the garden to eat.

Just as she sat down Max appeared.

'Oh, sorry, didn't realise you were eating. That looks nice. Just came to say thanks for looking after the place. How's things?'

Magda had to take pity on him. He was looking so beseechingly at the plate of food, that before she even realised, she was offering to make him some.

'That would be splendid.'

He followed her inside as she placed hers inside the oven to keep warm, removing the salad from the plate before doing so and set about preparing the same for Max. He talked about the conference and how well he had been received. Magda liked that he wasn't bragging at all but being straightforward and honest, even about the speakers he thought were better than he was.

They took the food back outside and Magda found herself telling him about Adrian Taylor-Beaumont.

Max was very interested, especially about the airfield. 'Yes, there was a small one here, but it closed years ago, just as Linda said. I guess he's from the one at Wittering. That's still operational as far as I know. You seem to have a bit of a liking for this chap. What's he got that I haven't then?'

Magda blushed.

'Oh no, it's nothing like that. I'm intrigued that's all. He seems so sad and almost lost. I just want to find out where Maria is now and then he can go and see her.'

But Magda wasn't sure now that this was quite honest on her part. There was something appealing about the man. He was very attractive, and yes, different. She couldn't put her finger on it, but he was old fashioned, polite, not as men were these days, more like her father's generation. She guessed that was because he was in the forces. The discipline and everything probably made them that way. And there was no getting away from it, he was exceedingly handsome. Maria was a lucky woman!

After they had eaten Magda went in and got them a plate of ice-cream each. She also brought out glasses of wine.

The evening was still and calm and the scent of the roses wafted over to the table, mixing with the scent of Lavender from the large bushes at side of the garden. *Oh my God!* Magda suddenly thought – *Lavender – Lavender Cottage. I wonder if that's what this was called until the grandson inherited it.*

'Max, was this place called Lavender Cottage before Mrs Grigson's grandson had it?'

'No, certainly not. It's been Hornbeams for as long as I've been here which is fourteen years this year.'

So that wasn't the answer.

Max continued to tease her about her *mystery man* until admitting that he was tired Max thanked her for the meal, kissed her on each cheek, and vaulted back over the fence.

Magda cleared up, started the dishwasher, made a cup of tea, and giving the dogs a biscuit each, went up to bed. She didn't feel like watching television or reading. She simply lay there thinking about the pilot and his search for Maria. She hoped Linda might throw some light on it once she had seen her mother in law. *I mustn't get obsessed with this*, she told herself sternly as she drifted into sleep.

Chapter Six

THE dream came again with a vengeance. Same things, running down the lane, people after her, feeling afraid, but more afraid for someone who was in danger up above. The shouts were menacing and hoarse behind her and she could hear them gaining on her as she ran. Her heart was thumping and she struggled to get breath into her lungs. She just knew she couldn't give up. If she stopped, they would get her – kill her!

Then the name popped into her head Adrian; it was Adrian who was in danger.

Magda woke to the sound of the dogs barking. God that was a new part, the feeling she would be killed. She looked at the clock which read ten to three. It was dark, no moon.

The dogs continued with their barking and Rollins was scratching at the door to get out. *Oh My God, is there someone in the house?* She lay there with her heartbeats matching those of the dream. She couldn't hear anyone but the dogs continued to go mad. After a few minutes, and knowing she would not get back to sleep she got up and took them downstairs. Aymes raced under the kitchen table and curled into a ball while Rollins jumped and scratched at the back door barking as he did so. With trepidation Magda opened it and he disappeared off down the garden.

Magda looked over to see if there was a light on at Max's. If there had been, she would have knocked on his door, she was so spooked. Rollins barked and barked and grabbing her borrowed torch, Magda put it on and walked down the garden. She gasped and shrank back as she saw a shape, a human shape, near the wall.

'Who's there? I'm calling the police.'

She went to turn back to go inside when a voice stopped her in her tracks. 'Maria?'

Turning she saw her mystery man, Adrian, this time not in uniform but wearing the raincoat that he had worn the first time. He was walking towards her with his arms outstretched.

'Maria?' he called again but as he got closer, he realised his mistake. I'm so sorry, for a moment there I thought you were someone else.'

'No, it's me Magda from the cottage.'

Magda once again recognised the intense sadness in his eyes. It called to her and resonated deep within her heart. It was the same intense sadness she felt if she thought about Dennis for too long. She wished now more than ever, that she could help this poor lost man to find his Maria. She was certain she must have been the love of his life.

'Would you like to come in Adrian? It's the middle of the night. I wish I knew where Maria was. Do you know her last name? If you can tell me, I could look for her on the internet?'

He gazed at her solemnly without speaking and she began to feel a bit uneasy. Then suddenly he spoke. 'Colleano. It's Colleano; Maria Colleano. Are you sure she doesn't live here?'

'Yes absolutely. I asked my neighbours. They don't know her.'

She wondered whether to tell him about Linda, but didn't want to get his hopes up. 'Look you're welcome to come in for a cup of tea.'

He didn't respond to her offer but just looked at her blankly before, raising his hand in farewell and walking off into the night. *What a strange man!* Magda thought as she waited for Rollins to come back in. She had to admit though, she was intrigued and yes possibly falling a little bit in love with him. He called to her, to everything in her that was loving and passionate. As before she thought *Maria is such a lucky girl. To have a man like that's love and devotion would be something very, very special.*

The next few days were very quiet. No nocturnal visits from the mystery man, no bad dreams. Beth came to visit instead of Magda going back to Highgate because Magda wanted Beth to see the place.

Beth immediately fell in love with the cottage and surroundings. 'Oh, it's no wonder you love living here, it's beautiful.' She went on to tell Magda how much she missed her and the dogs. 'Oh, and that Jeannie Axelrod. I've never known anyone quite so rude and brash. I really don't like her. Her husband is nice though. He came down and helped me change a light bulb in the lounge the other day. She, on the other hand, I avoid like the plague. So lovely when you and your dear husband lived there. Never mind, things change. That's one thing I've learnt in all my years on this earth.'

Magda was sad when at around five o'clock she asked her if she would mind taking her back. 'I get so tired these days, my dear,' she remarked sadly.

Magda had wanted her to meet Max and Janette, now they were both back with the latter a proud grandmother to baby Rose Louise but that wasn't now possible. Magda helped her friend into the car and they chatted inconsequentially until out of the blue Magda found herself telling Beth all about her mysterious stranger.

Unsurprisingly, Beth was intrigued. 'The poor man; he does sound sad.'

Magda then remembered that Maria's surname was Colleano and that she hadn't yet looked for her on the net. *I'll get onto it tomorrow* she thought as she dropped Beth back at Highgate. As when she had collected her, Magda felt a pang at seeing her old home; so familiar and yet now it felt as if she had never lived anywhere but Hornbeams.

The next morning, when she had finished breakfast, she got the dogs ready and walked them down to the garage, to pay her paper bill. At first she was disappointed to see only a man in there but, as she was paying, Linda emerged from the back, with a boxful of crisps in her arms.

'Hello there love. Jim this is the lady that was asking about the old airfield, do you remember? We asked his mum the other day when we visited and yes, there was one here in the war, but it was closed not long after the war ended. I asked mum about the cottages and she said she thought something happened there, but she couldn't remember for the life of her what it was. Sorry she couldn't be more help. She said you could go and see her if you wanted. She might be able to tell you something else. Between you and me I think she'd just like a bit of company.' Linda winked.

Magda thanked her and her husband, paid her bill and walked back home.

Back in her study, she booted up the computer and typed in the name Maria Colleano. There were a couple of hits but for people living in Italy, obviously not the one she sought. Then she typed in Hornbeams and was taken to the property site of the agents that had sold her the property. Next she tried Lavender Cottage but there was nothing. Feeling deeply frustrated she typed in the name Adrian Taylor-Beaumont.

There were several hits and she clicked on the first which detailed the holder of a Distinguished Flying Cross, a Second World War pilot giving details of some of the operations he had flown. Magda found herself getting really excited until she realised the dates were all wrong for the Adrian she had met. *Of course*, she thought, *could have been his father or even grandfather, possibly*. At the end of the article it gave a date of death a few years before. *So definitely not my one*. She felt disappointed. She tried the other listings, but they were much like the first. She knew there were genealogy sites but had no idea how to use them and anyway, she would need things like dates and places of birth which she didn't have.

Frustrated and disappointed she abandoned the computer in favour of sitting outside with the crossword and a cup of coffee. However, as she tried to solve the clues, she felt her mind wandering back to Adrian Taylor-Beaumont. It was unusual for fathers to name their sons after themselves in this day and age, so it must just be a coincidence. She tried in vain to banish the subject from her mind. Instead she remembered every detail of his handsome face, his beautiful eyes, long slim fingers and most of all the sadness in his eyes. *I wish I could locate Maria*, she thought yet again. Something in her wanted more than anything to make him happy, to take away that sadness. She wondered about the strong effect he was having on her. She didn't know him from Adam but still felt as if he had burrowed deep into her soul.

Just then she heard a cheery voice calling from over the fence, and looking up, saw Janette smiling and waving. 'Hello, got room for a granny to sit down? One who's going to bore you with loads of photos?'

'Yes, of course. Come through. I'll get you a coffee.' Smiling she gave Janette a hug. 'Congratulations and how is little Rose?'

'Oh, she's amazing. Beautiful of course and actually, so far, a very good little baby.'

Once they were both seated with coffee in front of them, Janette began to show her the photos. Magda thought the little girl looked like every other baby, but made the appropriate cooing noises and exclamations of 'Lovely' when required.

Janette was so excited that it made Magda very happy for her. They began to chat about other things, including Max and whether or not the Griffiths had returned since the dinner party. Magda said Max had been his usual lovely self and that she had not seen sight nor sound of the weekend family.

Janette laughed. 'You wait until the start of the school holidays. They'll be here in all their glory then. Skateboards up and down the lane. Music blaring, cars revving. You name it, you'll hear it believe me.'

The thought of such goings on horrified Magda and she said so. 'Oh God, I don't think I could bear it.'

'Come on love, chin up, it'll be for two to four weeks max. Then back to normal when they jet off to Antigua or Barbados or wherever it is they fancy.' Magda looked so crestfallen that Janette suggested they share a bottle of wine. 'I know it's early, but we can wet the baby's head.'

Smiling, Magda agreed and went inside to open one.

After a second glass Magda found herself talking to Janette about Adrian Taylor-Beaumont. It was a relief to be able to do so and when she finally ran out of steam Janette remarked, 'Golly, he's certainly made an impression, hasn't he? Bit strange though, don't you think, hanging around in the middle of the night? You need to be careful. Good job I'm back now to keep an eye on you. I know it's quiet here but serial killers can be anywhere you know?'

Magda was shocked and to be honest a little annoyed. 'Oh God no, he's nothing like that. If you met him, you'd see. He's just someone who's very lost and missing someone he loves. I'm sure he doesn't mean any harm to anyone. I know it seems odd the time he was here and everything, but honestly he's no threat. It's just incredibly sad really.'

Janette continued to look sceptical. 'If you say so. Of course, I've never met the man but I only meant be careful and if you're worried at all call me or Max. Here have you got your phone? Let me put our numbers in it for you.'

Magda knew her friend was looking out for her but was disappointed by the response. Wordlessly she went in to get her mobile, and when she returned Janette entered both names and numbers as promised.

'Look I'm sure you're right and he means no harm. It's just I know we're a bit isolated out here and we do all stick together. When the old lady was here, both Max and I kept an eye on her. That's how we are here.'

Magda thanked her. She knew Janette meant well. The thing was she hadn't been frightened by Adrian as soon as she had realised who it was standing in her garden. Instinct told her he would do her no harm.

After the wine, Janette left and Magda went back inside. She turned on the computer and googled Adrian Taylor-Beaumont again. *It can't be, but it seems such a coincidence*, she thought. *Both of them in the air force, both with such a distinguished sounding name.* But however she looked at it, the dates were all wrong and of course it said he was dead, which she knew for sure wasn't true.

The rest of the day was uneventful. She took the dogs for a long walk in the afternoon, made herself a meal and ate it at the garden table. The night was beautiful, the birds were going to sleep and the air was smooth and still, like velvet. Bats swooped and whirled in the garden, not coming near her.

Suddenly Aymes got to his feet and with hackles raised started growling.

'Don't be silly, they're only bats.' Magda got to her feet and walked over to calm him, just as she spotted Adrian at the gate.

This time he did not ask for Maria. He simply stayed and chatted for a while, refusing the refreshments Magda offered. She asked about his father, and whether he too had been in the air force but he laughed and said 'No'. He was easy to talk to but the cloak of sadness remained.

Magda wondered if she should bring up the subject of the woman he was so keen to be reunited with, but something stopped her. She liked to see him sitting opposite her, it felt right somehow. Once again, she offered a glass of wine, and once more he declined. She didn't like to go in and just get one for herself; felt awkward about doing so. And she didn't want to break the spell he seemed to be casting over her and over the evening.

They chatted on for over an hour, before he rose to leave, holding out his hand for her to shake. When she did an icy cold shiver ran up her spine. the feeling reminding her of the police knocking on her door in Highgate to tell her of her husband's death. Quickly she dismissed that, telling Adrian to call again any time.

He thanked her and as he walked through the gate, raised his hand in what was becoming for Magda an increasingly familiar gesture of farewell.

Magda went in for the wine and sat back down lost in thought. She was drawn to this man, of that there was no doubt. But it's too soon, she told herself. *The heart doesn't bother about things like that* came unbidden into her head as if someone had spoken the words aloud. All she knew was that she wanted desperately for him to call round again. Whistling for the dogs, she went inside and got ready for bed.

She fell asleep almost immediately but the dream came back, more real than ever. This time though, it was different. As she ran, she was aware of a woman running alongside her. The woman was panting and appeared absolutely terrified. She was wearing a long white nightgown and her thick black hair, which streamed in waves down her back, was blowing with the wind and the exertion of her running. She was shouting something but Magda couldn't hear her. The woman's mouth was opening but her words were unintelligible.

Magda was very afraid, even more so than when she had the dream previously.

There was shouting behind them; the sound of running feet. Male voices shouting terrible things; 'Whore – Traitor' were just two words that she could make out.

The woman turned round towards Magda and Magda's heart missed a beat. She was so beautiful. She had a heart shaped face with dark brown eyes and black hair. Her mouth was full and wide, with naturally rose-coloured lips. There was also something else about her, a sense of goodness, of serenity, although now she was terrified and it showed.

As Magda found the courage to turn to face the pursuing men, she realised the girl was no longer there.

Next thing she woke up. As before her heart was pounding; she was shaking and sweating. On the periphery of her vision she thought for a moment the girl from the dream was in the room. She caught the shape of her in the corner, the long nightgown, the black hair, the full lips. As she made to sit up the vision blurred and disappeared, leaving Magda with the most overwhelming sense of sadness she had ever experienced. Worse even than when she had lost Dennis. Not just sadness, more like extreme melancholy. She felt it like a weight on her chest and in her head.

From under the bed she heard a low growl, much like the one Aymes had given earlier in the garden. She moved across and looked down under the bed. There he was with risen hackles again, shivering and whimpering.

Getting out of bed, Magda wriggled under to try to calm him, as Rollins began to lick her bare feet but Aymes was not going to be coaxed out. Abandoning this and all thoughts of sleep, Magda got up and went downstairs. She let Rollins out into the garden, and put the kettle on to make a cup of tea.

The night outside was so still, but not with the usual welcoming feel. This felt more like it was holding its breath, waiting for something; something to happen. It felt eerie and unnerving.

Rollins raced back in and Magda bent to lay her face on his soft head. 'What's up with your brother, little boy?' she murmured, grateful for the warmth and feel of the little dog. Taking two biscuits from a container, she gave one to the waiting Rollins, and together with her mug of tea took the other upstairs for Aymes.

Eventually, motivated by the lure of the biscuit, he condescended to emerge. He took the biscuit and as soon as he had devoured it, wriggled right down under the duvet, where he lay, making a hump in the bed.

Luckily, she did not have the dream again when she returned to sleep but she awoke exhausted and still profoundly disturbed. For the first time since coming to the cottage, she did not want to get out of bed. She looked all around the room, but found nothing. There was no woman hiding in the corner, no strange, enigmatic, nocturnal male visitor but still she was unable to shake the sense of growing unease.

Eventually she swung her legs over the side of the bed, and putting on her dressing gown made her way downstairs. She opened the back door and this time both dogs flew out happily, barking with anticipation of what they might find outside. When they came back in, Magda prepared their breakfast and her own.

Once again, as the day was hot so she ate outside. She took her book and tried very hard to concentrate on the story. This however, proved impossible. All she could think about was Adrian and the woman from the dream.

She was very glad when Max popped his head over the fence and asked if she needed anything from the garage. Telling him 'No' at first, she then suggested he wait for her to get ready so she could go too with the dogs. 'I need to take them out, and it would be good to have some company.'

She felt so easy with Max and was pleased when he immediately agreed. 'Give me a shout when you're ready to go.'

Magda had a quick shower and pulled on a light cotton sun dress. She grabbed her sandals and quickly pinned her hair up in an untidy knot at the back of her head. As she was looking in the mirror, she felt, for a split second as if someone was behind her. In fact, she could have sworn she caught a glimpse of a face, a face she recognised from the night before. When she looked up all that was there was the wardrobe reflected in her dressing table mirror. *Stop it* she chided herself, *you're just getting too fanciful, it must be spending too long on your own.* Resolutely she banished all thought of the woman and of Adrian from her mind as she ran downstairs and out into the garden.

Together she and Max walked down to the garage and shop. Max was chatting about the upcoming college vacation. He was looking forward to going to Corsica for his holiday.

'I say why don't you come with me?' he surprised her suddenly by asking. 'We'd have a great time and the break would do you good. Janette was telling me about this man that's been hanging around. Like she said, you can't be too careful. If I were you, I'd give him his marching orders. Tell him you don't know this Maria woman and that you'll call the police if he keeps on hanging around.'

Magda felt furious for a split second but then realised that like Janette, Max was only looking out for her and that she was lucky to have such good friends and neighbours. She was touched too that he would want her to accompany him on his holiday although she knew she wouldn't go. She couldn't bring herself to leave Hornbeams now and there were the dogs to consider. She thanked him and said how much she appreciated the offer, but that she needed to stay at home and finish sorting out the cottage.

He smiled wryly at her, knowing, she felt sure, that she didn't want to be away if Adrian might visit.

Magda went on to offer to keep an eye on his cottage and of course to water his plants, both inside and out.

'That's lovely of you, and yes, I'll take you up on that. However, I would rather have had your company. Never mind, if you're sure. It's both our losses. I think we could have had an amazing time you know. Did you know Corsica is the birthplace of Napoleon?'

'Actually, I did and I would love to visit one day. It's just that now's not the right time.'

'Okay, have it your way. Stay and wait for your stalker.'

Magda could see by the gleam in his eye that he was joking and shrugged off the comment, batting him playfully on the arm. 'I know you and Janette are just being kind, but honestly this man doesn't mean me any harm. I feel it in my bones. Next time I'll knock for you if you're in and you can meet him. You'll soon see that he's harmless and that he's just terribly sad.'

By now they had reached the river and Magda let the dogs off the lead, to race around and jump in and out of the water.

Max contemplated her solemnly. 'Just be careful. That's all I'm saying. I feel you're a bit vulnerable now, what with all you went through earlier in the year.'

Magda smiled and took hold of his hand. 'Thank you Max. I'm lucky to be here and have such good friends.'

'And you'll wish you had taken me up on the offer once the Griffiths kids get here.'

He arched a wry eyebrow and once again Magda made as if to hit him, but he dodged and ran off, calling to the dogs as he did so.

Magda offered Max some lunch when they got back, but he said he had some marking to do and would take a rain check. They said goodbye at the gate, and she walked back inside.

The day was very hot so she decided to make do with just a cheese and tomato sandwich and a cup of tea. She fed the dogs and curled up on the sofa in the kitchen by the open window. She must have dozed for the next thing she knew she was back in the same nightmarish dream. She was running again, panting, with beating heart, dry mouth and perspiration pouring off her. The danger was so close, it was almost palpable. Once again, the young woman was running alongside of her and this time Magda realised that it was her fear she was experiencing. With a lightning bolt of clarity, hitherto unfelt, she knew also with absolute certainty, that this woman was Maria, the Maria Adrian sought so desperately. In the world of her dream Magda reached out to her. She wanted to tell her everything would be alright, that Adrian loved her. She reached over to touch the woman's shoulder and as her hand made contact, she was jerked unceremoniously awake. Breathless and feeling winded, she lay there unmoving despite the discomfort of her cooling sweat.

So, that was Maria; that beautiful, frightened and troubled woman was Maria!

Magda felt scared. *Why am I having these dreams? What is going on? Am I going mad? No,* she reasoned. *If I was I certainly wouldn't be worrying about it. I'd be oblivious to the fact. What was it then?* It was as if this woman, this Maria wanted something from her. Wanted to make contact through dreams. *But why?* Magda reasoned that the key to this must lie with Adrian. Then something frightening, something black and horrifying entered her mind. *Is it the house? Is there something here in this house that dark and disturbing?* She thought about what Beth had said, and about Aymes being scared and hiding. He hadn't ever done that in Highgate.

But the cottage felt peaceful and welcoming. She had felt at home since the first time she visited and was shown around. She had known that this was where she was meant to be.

Still feeling shaky, she got up and went to make another cup of tea, the previous one being stone cold. As the kettle boiled, she reached into a cupboard and took out the half bottle of brandy she had bought the other day. When she had poured the tea, she added a good slug of brandy to it and took the mug outside, to sit in the sun. She drank the alcohol-laced tea but it didn't cure how shaken and agitated she felt.

Rollins came outside and curled up in the dog bed she had placed near her chair but yet again there was no sign of Aymes. Magda rose and went in search of him. This time she found him in her bed. He seemed fine though, not shivering or looking anxious. He didn't want to get up or come downstairs, so she left him there.

All day she felt twitchy and unable to settle. She did a bit of gardening, made herself a chicken casserole for dinner and at around five o'clock made another cup of tea, which once again, she laced with a generous slug of brandy. She found her mobile and thought about calling Max and asking if he would like to join her for dinner. She was about to press the number when she hesitated, thinking she shouldn't become reliant on his cheerful good nature to help her get over her anxieties.

Instead she called Janette but there was no answer. She wondered if her friend had gone back to visit baby Rose.

When the phone shrilled she jumped in alarm.

It was a former work friend asking if she would like to go to a colleague's retirement party. Magda had liked Graham, the gentle psychiatrist that had led their team. The party was three weeks away and Magda told her friend she would think about it and let her know. They chatted for a while and then she excused herself because she could smell the casserole which she thought must be ready. She cooked some green beans to accompany it and then took her plate out to the table in the garden. The casserole was good, but she found she didn't really have much appetite. She ate what she could and placed the remainder in a container to freeze for another day. She ate an apple for dessert and placing the dirty dishes in the dishwasher, poured a small amount of brandy into a glass and went back to sit outside.

She stayed there feeling the gentle twilight beginning to wrap her in its velvety coat. It was strangely peaceful as the bats returned, swooping down and then back up into the darkening sky. The call of an owl and the shriek of a fox sent her inside for more brandy. When she returned mere moments later, Adrian was standing on the path just inside the gate.

'Hello.' He greeted her warmly.

'Hello, how are you?' Magda felt her heart lighten at his presence.

He smiled. 'I am very well, and yourself?' He spoke with a strange formality, like someone from an earlier time.

Assuring him she was well, she asked if he would like to sit and have a drink. Much to her pleasure he took one of the chairs opposite her at the table, but refused refreshment. As the night sky deepened from indigo to black he began to talk. He told her he was a pilot in the Royal Air Force. His family came from Wiltshire where they owned a small country estate. And he was unmarried.

Magda listened to his voice enthralled by the upper-class inflection and his ease of speech. Suddenly, more than anything, she wanted to touch the long-fingered hand that rested on the table as he spoke. She blushed and was glad of the cover of darkness. He was so polite, not at all suggestive and she felt ashamed of the sensual feelings she was experiencing as she watched and listened to him talk. She felt like a teenager again. *Was he going to touch her? Kiss her?* She hoped so, more than she could have imagined.

After about an hour, though, he got up and said he had to leave. She wanted to stop him, to put out a hand and halt his movement. She did nothing though, simply smiled and told him she had enjoyed his company and that he was welcome to call again any time.

He walked slowly down the path, and at the gate turned and raised his hand in salutation before disappearing into the darkness.

Magda remained standing, staring after him and then shocked felt something like a push in the back. She jumped at the hiss of a voice. Had he returned? No this was something else, a female voice. It harshly spat, out words she was unable to make out.

Then, like a bolt from the blue, Aymes ran barking through the garden before returning to Magda's side where he leaned right into her as close as he was able. Absentmindedly she patted his head as she felt him quiver beside her.

The voice had gone as quickly as it came.

Chapter Seven

SHE did not dream that night and when she woke in the morning her mind immediately went to Adrian and the conversation they had shared the previous evening. Once again she was struck by how sad he seemed and saw reflected in him her own sorrow. She went downstairs and found the last photograph she had taken of Dennis. It was taken not long before he died. They had gone out for a celebratory meal with a few friends and this was one her friend Veronica had taken of the two of them together. She marvelled at how happy they had looked and that neither had any idea of what fate held in store.

The day passed rather slowly. Magda telephoned Janette but there was no reply. In the afternoon she took the dogs for a long walk along the river, returning home feeling tired. She fed them, made herself an omelette and some French bread. Just as she had finished she heard the gate open and close and her heart missed a beat.

There he was standing just inside, looking at her hesitantly. This time he was wearing his full air force uniform and Magda thought how uncomfortably hot he must feel in it on such a warm airless evening.

She smiled and said simply 'Hello.'

He walked up the path and sat where he had the previous evening. Once again they chatted for a long time but as before he refused every offer of refreshment and when it was time to leave, despite her rising to be closer, he did not kiss her as she hoped he might.

This time she walked down the path with him and watched as he walked off, calling out a goodbye as he turned to give his usual salutation.

'First signs so they say.' A cheery voice came from outside the gate and there was Max looking at her and laughing.

'Sorry?'

'First signs of madness, talking to yourself.'

'But I wasn't, I was…'

And Magda realised that Adrian was in fact nowhere in sight, despite having been there a moment ago.

Laughing Max climbed over the fence into her garden. 'How about a glass of wine for a fellow, who might do some serious damage to a student if he has to speak to one ever again?'

Magda laughed, despite feeling disconcerted about where Adrian had gone.

'Bad day?'

'The worst. Some students just don't get it that if you don't do the work, you don't pass exams, simple as that. Then I become the bad guy, because they've failed and will have to tell their parents. And these are meant to be the elite of the educable world!'

Max sighed theatrically which Magda ignored, walking inside to get the wine.

They sat drinking and chatting for about an hour until Magda started yawning.

'Am I boring you?' Max said that with another of his typical laughs.

'Oh god no, so sorry. I just suddenly felt terribly weary. Don't know why. I haven't exactly been doing much today, or any day recently for that matter.'

'Oh yes, did Janette tell you about the job?'

'Job? No what job? Actually, I haven't seen her for a few days. I assumed she'd gone back to visit Rose.'

'No, she's around. Think she's just been busy with work. She was looking for you the other day. They're advertising for a counsellor at her work, part-time, I think. She wondered if you might be interested.'

Magda said she liked the idea, unsure if she was ready to enter the real-life world of work despite thinking the very opposite only a day or two before. 'Thanks Max. I'll give her a ring. It might be too soon for me, but I wouldn't mind knowing a bit about it.'

Max leant over and took one of her hands in his. 'Sorry. I keep forgetting you've been bereaved so recently. You seem so together. Nothing like my mum when she lost my dad. Oh god, sorry again, I didn't mean that to come out the way it sounded. It's just that you have an ease about you and a calm. I guess that's your training coming into play. If you ever want to talk about…Dennis, wasn't it? Your husband, I'm always here with a willing ear.'

He seemed so sincere. Magda felt very lucky to have him as a friend and neighbour. He continued to hold her hand, but it didn't feel as if he was making a pass or anything clumsy like that. It felt as if he was being a true friend.

'Thank you, Max, that's very kind. Actually, I haven't really spoken about Dennis much at all. It's almost as if it hasn't happened, and wasn't real. It's strange. At the funeral I'm sure both his mother and sister felt I was heartless as I wasn't weeping and wailing as they were. I just felt numb and have done ever since really. Maybe that does make me heartless, I don't know?'

'Grief affects everyone differently, but you'll know that more than anyone. Don't beat yourself up about it. Feeling numb could be a way of protecting yourself. I meant it though, if ever you do want to talk then, please do. Now I'm going to go and let you get some sleep.'

Max kissed her lightly on the cheek before getting up and leaping over the fence. With a quick wave and a 'Night, night, sleep well,' he was gone.

Magda picked up the glasses, took them inside and left them in the sink. She gave the dogs a little biscuit and went upstairs to get ready for bed. As before, when she looked in the mirror, she had that same sense that there was a shadowy presence standing behind her. It was a feeling more than anything. She splashed some cold water on her face, telling herself not to be stupid, put on her nightie and got into bed.

The following morning, refreshed and invigorated, Magda had her breakfast and went to pay her paper bill.

Linda who was working that morning chatted for a while and then told her where her mother-in-law lived in the care home. 'We went to see her yesterday and she said she remembered something about the cottages. She'd love you to visit her and said she could tell you all about it.'

Magda took the piece of paper with the address that Linda held out to her and decided she would go the following day.

When she reached her cul-de-sac, she spotted a huge people carrier with a trailer parked outside the unoccupied cottage. This must be the Griffiths, here for the holidays, she thought with a grimace as she registered the booming bass sounds coming from the back garden.

Just then Emily Griffiths emerged round the side and waved hesitantly to her. Magda, not wanting to appear as unfriendly as she actually felt about having her peace and quiet disrupted, waved back. A tall teenager appeared behind his mother. Magda watched in amazement as the boy took some of his things from the car boot and piled them into his mother's arms. He then removed what looked like a sleeping bag which he carried in behind her.

How awful, thought Magda and *how absolutely right Max and Janette were saying they were brats.* They had to take after their father.

Emily emerged again looking flustered, this time with a teenage girl in tow. The girl waved across at Magda and gave a rather sweet smile. She was very like her mother, small, pretty, fair but unremarkable. Magda walked over to greet them both.

'Hello Emily, you must be here for the holidays.' She smiled at the girl. 'I'm Magda, I live in that cottage there.'

The girl smiled shyly. 'I'm Gemma. Yes we come for a month every summer holidays. Cool dogs. Would it be okay to stroke them?'

'Oh yes, they'd love it, they love a fuss.'

Gemma bent down and stroked the two little dogs who went into ecstasy at this unexpected treat. Aymes rolled onto his back with his legs in the air and Gemma got down onto the dusty road, oblivious to the fact that she was wearing pristine white shorts. She tickled and stroked them for ages, as Magda tried to make conversation with Emily. As before this was rather heavy going as most of Emily's answers were monosyllabic. It was as if she didn't feel she really had the right to talk openly which set Magda's counsellor antenna twitching and she wondered about domestic abuse within the household.

Just then the boy sauntered outside again. 'Dad wants to know where the beer is? He said he bought some earlier at that little village shop.' He did not even deign to acknowledge Magda's presence.

'It's in the fridge, I saw it. Come and look at these dogs, Jus.' Gemma called across but he ignored her, turning back towards the house.

'I apologise for my brother; he's a twat.'

Gemma had got up from the ground, and wiping her hands down the sides of her shorts, which did not improve their now rather dirty state, she smiled at Magda. 'He thinks he's cool and everything, since he turned sixteen and will be going into sixth form next term.'

Magda instinctively liked Gemma. She was bright and open, and up close was actually very pretty indeed.

Gemma hesitated for a second or two before asking, 'Hey do you think I could take these little guys for a walk sometime? It might make up for the boredom of having to be here for the next three weeks.'

Magda explained that they might be shy and that it would probably be better if Gemma accompanied them on their walk and that would give the dogs the time to get to know her.

'That's cool. How about tomorrow? I can get up early if you want. What time do you usually go?'

Magda smiled at Gemma's enthusiasm. 'Well I don't get up that early these days, so how about we say eleven? Would that suit you?'

'Yes, eleven would be great. Thanks. I'd better go and help mum. See you tomorrow.' And with a final pat of the dogs and a wave to Magda, Gemma raced back inside.

The girl's delightful, Magda thought. Nothing like either of her parents, although physically she bore a strong resemblance to her mother. She went back to her own cottage smiling. Gemma was a breath of fresh air. When she got inside, she remembered that she had planned to visit Jim's mother tomorrow at the care home. *Oh well I can go in the afternoon*, she thought. She wondered if it would be all right just to arrive, but came to the conclusion that she ought to phone first to make sure.

'Have you got satnav, only it's a bugger to find the first time?' Linda had told her. She found the piece of paper that Linda had given her. The care home was called *The Willows Guest House* and was in a place called Ramsey Forty Foot.

When the phone was answered it was by a rather haughty sounding lady but when Magda asked if it would be all right to visit Mrs Cooper the following afternoon, the lady's tone lightened immediately. 'Oh yes, Margaret would love a visit. Are you the lady her daughter in law was speaking about? She's really looking forward to meeting you.'

Magda said 'Yes, that's me. I'll be at the home around three if that's okay.'

The lady gave her name as Caroline Conroy, said that she was the home's owner and that three o'clock would be fine.

'I'd like to bring Mrs. Cooper something. Is there anything she likes in particular or anything she isn't supposed to have like chocolates?'

'Oh, Margaret loves chocolates and she's not diabetic or anything. In fact she's a very healthy lady apart from her arthritis. Bring anything. She'll just be delighted and probably more with your company than anything else.'

Assuring Caroline that she would be there the following afternoon, Magda put down the phone. She went into the study and booted up her computer to look for the address so that she would at least have some idea how far it was. It looked to be about a forty-minute drive.

Hesitantly Magda hovered over the search engine, wanting once again to look for Adrian Taylor-Beaumont. *Stop it*, she berated herself mentally. *This is becoming an obsession.* Grudgingly she powered off the computer before she could give in to the impulse and went out into the garden to do some tidying.

She cut a large bunch of roses, which she took inside to put into a vase. Their perfume was heady and sweet and took her back to her childhood. Her mother had always grown roses in their little garden in the North London suburb where Magda had grown up. Her parents had both died in a car accident when Magda was just nineteen and away at university. As an only child, she had been totally bereft and for a while, until meeting Dennis, very lonely. The scent of the roses made her think of her parents and then of Dennis. She wondered why some people experienced so much loss in their lives while others very little.

This inevitably led her to think of Adrian and his Maria. She wanted more than anything to know their story but somehow something in Adrian's manner had so far stopped her from asking him to tell her about it. There was this sense of sadness, but also something else - an aloofness that made her feel he would think that she was prying. After all, she barely knew him. If he wanted to tell his story then he would. She just had to be patient. Always assuming that is, that she saw him again. Something deep inside told her that he would return, however. Of that, she was certain.

Chapter Eight

THE following afternoon, after she and Gemma had their promised walk together, which Magda had thoroughly enjoyed, she got ready to visit Mrs Cooper.

As she did so she reflected on Gemma and what a delightful girl she had proved to be. She was self-confident, and very funny. She kept Magda in fits of laughter talking about her *twat of a brother* and her embarrassing father. 'My God, he's so pompous' she had declaimed and as for her brother, well he went after *anything with a pulse*, deeming himself irresistible, which Gemma thought was hilarious. She didn't say very much about her mother, just that she really ought to, as she put it, 'Grow a pair.'

Magda had promised Gemma that they could walk together again soon and that maybe after that she could try taking the dogs out on her own without Magda to see how things went. Gemma was thrilled with that and as they said goodbye to each other at the gate, she had returned to give Magda a big hug before going inside.

Magda programmed the address of the care home into her satnav and started on the journey. She had cut another huge bunch of roses to give to Mrs Cooper and purchased a box of chocolates at the garage. There had been no sign of either Jim or Linda. Instead a rather taciturn teenager was manning the till. Magda had wondered if he was the paper boy, but had not enquired given the manner in which he glowered at her for interrupting his perusal of a car magazine when she had gone to pay.

The drive was a pleasant one, despite the still raging heat. She found the property easily enough as it was just set back on the main through road. It seemed a very isolated spot for a home but the view all around was beautiful and the home itself looked lovely. It was a large detached house made of stone, with gabled windows.

Magda parked on the drive outside and got out of her car. There were two or three elderly people sitting enjoying the garden and they greeted Magda with a cheery 'Hello' as she mounted the steps to the front door, noticing the ramp alongside the steps, obviously to give easy wheelchair access.

She walked into a high-ceilinged room, which at some point, would have been the hallway of the house. There was a reception desk to one side of the imposing ascent to the upper floors. It had a stair lift attached for the elderly, frailer inhabitants. Everywhere looked bright and welcoming and not at all clinical, apart from the ubiquitous smell of disinfectant, which Magda associated with hospitals.

There was a cheerful-looking, plump young lady behind the reception desk. Her badge announced her name as Gillian. She had bright red curly hair and the smile she bestowed upon Magda was one of genuine warmth and broadened further still when Magda told her she was there to visit Mrs Cooper.

'Oh yes, that's brilliant, we were told you were coming. She's very excited. Apart from her son and daughter-in-law she doesn't get many visitors. Are those for her?' Gillian indicated the flowers Magda was holding.

'Yes, they are. They're only from the garden I'm afraid, but I have brought these as well.' Magda indicated the chocolates she was carrying.

'Brill! She'll love those and I might even be offered one. Hang on I'll just let them know you're here.'

Magda was delighted by the girl's warm enthusiasm and thought fleetingly that when she was old, she wouldn't mind ending up somewhere like this.

Gillian reached for the telephone on the desk and Magda heard her tell someone on the other end 'Margaret's visitor's here.'

A few minutes later a tall, imposing woman, in her early sixties came down the stairs. 'Hello, Mrs McClean? I'm Caroline Conroy. Nice to meet you. You found us all right then?'

Magda shook hands and assured Mrs Conroy that she had.

'Margaret's very excited about your visit. It's probably harder for her than a lot of our residents as she has all her faculties and is in good health and very mobile still. Follow me. She's out in the back garden. I'll bring you both some tea in a moment.'

She led the way through the house out into a beautiful back garden. On the far side of the terrace, sat a small, white-haired lady, holding a magazine. Mrs Conroy spoke gently to her. 'Margaret, your visitor's here.'

Margaret Cooper looked up and smiled. She caught sight of Magda and grabbing a pretty, floral coloured walking stick, tried to rise.

Magda, sensing her discomfort, gently pushed her back to a sitting position. 'Please don't get up Mrs Cooper.'

'Oh, thank you my dear, the old bones are not what they were, and do please call me Margaret.'

She had the bluest eyes Magda had ever seen. Her face was apple-cheeked and criss-crossed with wrinkles but her eyes twinkled in friendliness and delight. Magda thought she must be in her late eighties if not older. Her hands were gnarled and misshapen, with huge knuckle joints that were red and swollen. She patted the chair next to her, exclaiming in delight when Magda handed her the flowers and chocolates. 'Oh, how lovely of you, my dear. You are most kind, although having your visit would have been enough. Did you grow the lovely roses yourself?'

Magda told her that they were indeed from the garden, but that she could not take credit for them, as there were already in place when she moved in.

Margaret, smiled and exclaimed delightedly again as she took the chocolates. 'Oooh look, thank you. Caroline, please take these and offer one to dear Gillian, will you?'

Mrs Conroy took the proffered box and with a smile and a pat to Margaret's shoulder, told her she would and that she would have some tea sent out.

When she had gone Margaret turned expectantly towards Magda. 'Linda said you wanted to know about the old airfield? It's not there now I'm afraid. It was used a lot in the war. Planes flying over all the time. Terrible noise, but they were defending us all so what could you do? I used to go up there sometimes when they had a dance on. There were some Americans there too, towards the end. Oh, what lovely young men. So generous too. They always had sweets and even nylons for some of the girls. Not that I would have accepted any of course. Not really the done thing, you know?'

Magda smiled. 'Do you remember anything about the cottages that were there? There's four of them and I live in the furthest one. Down by the river, not that far from your son's garage.'

'I know where you mean, my dear. Those cottages have been there forever, I would say.'

Margaret's reminiscence was interrupted by the arrival of a woman with a tea tray. Deftly she placed, cups, saucers, a teapot and plates onto the table with a shy smile. She put a little silver sugar bowl down and a plate of cakes. Magda thanked her and in heavily accented English she said 'Very welcome,' before turning back to go into the house.

'That's Vanya; she's Russian. She does the cooking for us. Such a sweet girl, but doesn't speak much English. Wonderful cook though.'

Magda was wondering how she might press Margaret more about the cottages.

'Would you mind dear, pouring the tea? My hands won't let me I'm afraid; bloody useless things.'

Magda spotted tears in Margaret's eyes so without hesitation she rose and poured them both a cup of tea. Neither wanted sugar but Margaret took one of the cakes. Magda didn't want to waste time and so she declined.

Margaret chewed thoughtfully before swallowing her piece of cake. 'There was trouble there, at one of those cottages, sometime during the war. Can't remember exactly, but it was something to do with a foreign girl who lived there.'

Magda gasped and held her breath waiting for Margaret to continue. At last was she going to find out about Maria. 'A foreign girl,' Margaret had said and Colleano was a foreign name; Spanish perhaps, Magda thought.

Margaret chewed another mouthful of cake, thoughtfully before speaking again. 'I think there was a fire, something like that. I never met the woman. Saw her once, pretty little thing she was. Not unlike you, dear. I heard in the village; yes, we had a village then with a school and everything. All seemed to die out in the fifties. You know after the war, there were opportunities for people. People moved away. The school closed down. It was a village store and post office where my Jim's garage and shop are now. Anyway, what was I saying? Oh yes, that foreign girl. Seems she was having a bit of a thing with one of the pilots. Don't know what happened; just that some men in the village took against her. Something to do with her being a foreigner, although I don't think she was German. At least nobody ever told us she was. Anyway, my mother knew all about it but wouldn't say what happened. I know it wasn't very nice though, that much I can tell you.'

Margaret seemed, suddenly to run out of steam. She finished her cake and yawned. 'Do you mind my dear, I'm suddenly very tired. Will you come and see me again? I've loved our little chat and remembering things about the village, as was. What do you think of that Linda? I never thought she was good enough for my Jim. He was always such a good boy. I lived with them for a long time, but then, what with the business and everything, I became a burden.'

Margaret yawned again.

'Yes of course I'll come again, if you'd like me to. I don't really know Linda, but she's very helpful in the shop. I'm afraid I only met Jim once, but he seems nice.'

Magda was finding it hard to hide her disappointment. She felt she had come so near to hearing about Maria, but in the end it amounted to nothing. although she liked Margaret and would indeed visit again.

'Shall I go and get Mrs Conroy for you? Or would you like me to help you inside? Are you going to go in and have a rest?'

'Yes, dear. Yes, if you wouldn't mind telling them inside that I'd like to go back to my room. Thank you so much for visiting and the lovely flowers and chocolates. Please do come again.'

Assuring Margaret that she would, she bent down to give her frail body a gentle hug, before leaving. A moment later when she turned back to wave she noticed Margaret's head was nodding as if she was falling asleep already.

Magda went in to find Gillian and tell her, 'Margaret would like to come in for a rest.'

'Okay, let me ring for somebody to come to help her. How did you get on? She's lovely isn't she? You'd never know she was ninety-two would you? Got all her marbles, if you know what I mean? Not like some of the poor souls here.'

Bidding her goodbye Magda left and walked down the steps to her car. On the way home she pondered the little she had learned. She was certain that the foreign girl must be Maria, but it didn't make sense. If she had been in the war she would be elderly by now. Adrian was no more than thirty-five at the most. Surely, he would not be seeking a woman of Maria's age. Unless she was a relative rather than a girlfriend or lover as Magda had assumed. But no, he was so sad and so intense and she felt sure that there was a romantic element to their story. Unless, the woman, that Maria, was Adrian's Maria's mother? But that didn't make sense either. Why would he be looking for her mother so intently? And what about the fire? All in all, it seemed more confusing than ever. *I'll just have to bite the bullet and ask Adrian when he comes again*, she thought.

She arrived home to find Gemma waiting very obviously for her to come back.

'Hi,' she greeted the girl cheerily as she got out of her car.

'Hi Magda.' The two words were enough to reveal a totally different girl from the bubbly one who had walked with Magda and the dogs earlier. 'Is everything okay?'

To her consternation Gemma burst into tears.

'Oh Gemma, come on inside and tell me what's wrong.'

She shepherded the girl inside and both of them were given a riotous canine welcome. This managed to bring a smile to Gemma's face as she sniffed back her tears, bending down to stroke their silky heads.

A few minutes later, with a glass of apple juice and a biscuit in front of her, Gemma began to talk. She told Magda how much she hated her father and her brother and that her father often hit her mother and had done so again that afternoon. Wiping her eyes and nose with the back of her hand, Gemma sniffed and Magda handed her the box of tissues from the work surface.

'Oh, Gemma, you poor thing, and your poor mum too. I have to ask this, does he hit you or your brother too?'

Gemma shook her head.

'No, only mum, but he's given her a black eye before now. Mum always says she slipped in the shower or something equally lame, but I know dad did it and I saw him today. She hadn't brought the type of French mustard with us that he likes. She made some ham sandwiches for lunch and put ordinary mustard on them and he just lost it. Started shouting and bellowing like he does. Mum said she was sorry for forgetting to bring the one he likes and he swiped the back of his hand right across her face. I was just coming in the kitchen and saw him do it.'

Gemma began to sob again, burying her face into her crossed arms, as she leant on the kitchen table. Magda simply let her cry for a while. She had immediately slipped into counsellor mode and knew that the girl needed the release of tears.

In a bit, Gemma looked up and gave Magda a watery smile. 'Sorry. I probably shouldn't have told you. You won't tell anyone, or do anything will you?'

Magda reassured her that she wouldn't. 'Really the only person who can do anything about the situation is your mum. If he's that bad to her, she should consider her options and whether it would be better to leave him. She has to be the one to make that decision. It would be a different matter if he hit you, then I would need to inform someone. I believe you though, when you say he doesn't, so I'm not going to do anything but if your mum would like someone to talk to, then I am a trained counsellor and I'd be happy to listen to her. The same goes for you Gemma; you can tell me anything and talk to me anytime you want to. Not just when you're here. I'll give you my telephone number before you leave and you can ring me anytime. Now how about you drink up that juice, eat the biscuit and we take the dogs down to the river for a quick run?'

The idea of the walk brought a smile back to Gemma's face and she downed her apple juice hastily. The dogs were ecstatic at the thought of another walk and jumped around whilst Magda got their leads, handing them to Gemma to put on.

Gradually as they walked, Gemma began to regain her usual exuberance. She hugged the dogs goodbye on their return and then hugged Magda. 'Thanks Magda, you're ace. I've never spoken to anyone about this before. Well mum of course but she tries to pretend that what happens is normal. Thank you so much. We're here all next week. Is it okay if I come and walk the dogs?'

'Of course, it is. If you want to, now they know you, you could take them on your own sometimes. However, if you want to talk, I'll always come. And don't forget, you can talk to me anytime; anytime at all.'

Although she was worried for Gemma and for Emily, Magda was grateful for the problem because it stopped her from obsessing over Maria and Adrian.

She walked into her cottage and gave the dogs some fresh water. She made herself a meal, and as ever, took it outside. There was absolutely no sign of the weather breaking. Magda wondered if this was a record for Britain. Since living here, she hardly ever watched the news, and she only got the paper so that she could do the crossword. She didn't ever bother reading it but listening to Gemma had inspired her to think about returning to work and she walked over to Janette's cottage after her meal to see about the job Max had mentioned.

Janette was in and welcomed Magda with a glass of wine, which they took outside to make the most of the setting sun.

'The job's for eighteen hours each week at the same hospital I work at worked at in Huntingdon. It's a good hospital, but like everywhere these days, it has its fair share of problems. The psychological therapies department that you'd be in is a good one and the staff are great. You can fill in an application form on the NHS website. If you want to, put me down as a referee. I'd be happy to do a reference for you. I can tell you have the qualities that make a good counsellor.'

Magda felt tears threatening. There were still moments like this since losing Dennis, when a kind word made her feel emotional. She hugged Janette and thanked her, telling her she would apply.

'Brilliant. I hope you get it. We could go for lunch together too sometimes which would be great. Phil is the psychologist in charge. He'll love you I know. Let me know how you get on.'

Assuring her friend that she most certainly would, Magda took her leave and wandered back home. Once again, the bats were swooping around, the darkness was like velvet and there was a perfect crescent moon in the sky. Spotting one lone bright star, Magda felt as if it might be Dennis looking down on her to see that she was all right.

'I am, darling, but I miss you so much.' She whispered to the still, night sky.

Chapter Nine

MAGDA'S sleep was untroubled and she woke refreshed, ready for the day. She got up, let out the dogs and made breakfast. She heard a rap at the window as she was eating and turning saw Max grinning at her through the window. As she went to the back door to let him in, she became aware of music thumping out from the Griffiths' cottage. Looking up at the clock she saw it was only ten past nine, far too early for such a racket.

Max came loping in with a silly grin on his face. 'Told you the noise would be dreadful. You should have agreed to come to Corsica with me. That's why I'm here. No, don't panic, I'm not going to drag you with me kicking and screaming, I've come to give you these.' He waved a bunch of keys at her. 'That is if you're still up for watering the plants?'

'Of course, I am. Come in, sit down, have some coffee.'

Magda found a mug and poured coffee into it from the cafetière. She went to the fridge for milk, remembering that, unlike herself, he took his coffee white. They chatted for a while and Magda told him about the job.

'Sounds perfect, and eighteen hours a week; a good way to ease you back into the world of work.'

Suddenly Magda remembered in horror that she had forgotten about her friend's invitation to the leaving party at her old job. 'Oh my God, I've just remembered I was supposed to ring a friend about an invitation and it went clean out of my mind. There's been so much going on here, I totally forgot.'

Max was regarding her rather oddly. 'So much going on, in this quiet little hamlet?!'

She blushed, realising she had meant with Adrian. 'Oh you know, moving in, getting the cottage straight; meeting you and Janette, that sort of thing.' *Good save Magda*, she congratulated herself as she got up to pour more coffee. 'When are you off then?'

'This evening. Flight's at the crack of dawn tomorrow so staying overnight near Heathrow. Oh, the bliss of no students until the beginning of October.' Leisurely he stretched his arms above his head, balancing his chair on two legs.

Magda laughed. She was going to miss Max for the two weeks he would be away.

'Find out anything more about your air force chappie?' he surprised her by asking as he rose to leave.

'No, not really, but Linda at the shop - I went to visit her mother in law yesterday and she knew the airfield that was here. She also said something about a woman and a fire. Have you heard anything about that?'

'No. Like I said, all before my time here. I came here with wife number two, getting on for fifteen years ago now. I think I remember someone saying something about the old airfield, but no idea where it was. It could be where they built that little estate of houses. Way past the garage on the road to Ramsey. Don't even know what it was called, so can't help I'm afraid. Anyway, I don't want to encourage the competition!' This last uttered with his usual twinkling grin.

Magda saw him off. The noise from the Griffiths' was even louder if possible and the boy, Justin was leaning out of his bedroom window, smoking. Max saluted Magda as he jumped the fence, raising his eyebrows at both the noise and the boy.

Later on Gemma popped in to say she couldn't walk that day as her mother was taking her into Peterborough to get some clothes for their forthcoming holiday so Magda asked where they were going.

Gemma shrugged. 'The Maldives. It'll be boring and Mum and I will be left hanging on our own whilst Dad and Jus play sports and do things together. I wish we could stay here instead.'

She looked so crestfallen Magda felt very sorry for her. *Money isn't everything* she thought as she wished Gemma well for the shopping trip and told her they could walk the following day. She got the dogs ready and set off alone. En route she stopped at the garage to settle the paper bill and finding Linda in the shop, she told her about her visit the previous day.

'Oh brilliant. Margaret will have loved seeing you and chatting. I feel bad that we can't get there more often than we do. Did she tell you anything useful about the airfield?'

'Not really, but she said something about a fire and our cottages. Anyway, it was worth it. I'll probably go and visit her again. She got very tired though.'

'Yes, she does. She has Rheumatoid Arthritis, but other than that she's as fit as a flea, and has a very active mind. She does crosswords and puzzles, but is finding writing very hard these days. Jim's trying to persuade her to use an iPad. He bought her one for her birthday, but she's suspicious of it.'

Magda paid her bill and Linda informed her that *the boy* was on holiday for the next two weeks and that Jim would come up in his car to deliver the paper. 'He might be a bit late, I'm afraid, but he'll get to you eventually.'

'Oh no, don't worry, I can come down and get one.'

Linda would not hear of this. 'It's great for us to have regular customers. We deliver to three of those cottages although the gentleman in one of them is away then too. Jim's happy to come to deliver to you and next door.'

Thanking her and asking her to pass on her thanks to Jim, Magda left the shop and went outside. She untied the dogs and set off to the river. Now that all was quiet, she allowed herself to think about Adrian. She wondered when she might see him again, and hoped it would be sooner rather than later.

She had at least rung her friend to apologise for letting her down over the leaving party. She had been very understanding and told her it had been a bit of a damp squib anyway. Lots of people were on leave and Graham, who's party it was, had left early, not wanting the fuss.

Magda thought about the job and determined that she would apply online as soon as she got home. She began to reflect on how everything changes for everyone. It had been a theme amongst her clients and now she realised more than ever how true it was. This time last year, she had been preparing to go to Italy on holiday with Dennis, and the two of them had felt as if they hadn't a care in the world. Neither was to know just how swiftly their lives would change a few short months later.

Magda found that once again she missed Max being around. It felt lonely without him. Even though they didn't live in each other's pockets, she was grateful for the friendly presence he provided. She booted up her computer and searched the website for the job, found it and read the spec and application form. There was nothing she wasn't qualified to do and she began to complete it. Halfway through she was suddenly realised with piercing clarity that she didn't really want to be working now. She began to consider the pros and cons. She certainly didn't need the money, thanks to Dennis and the main argument in favour of getting a job was worrying that her preoccupation with Adrian and Maria was due to her having nothing except the little dogs in her life. At times it seemed unhealthy.

She shook herself and continued with the application. *After all*, she reasoned, *I may not get offered the job anyway, so why not just have a go and see?* She finished it, emailed it and then closed down the computer before she could be tempted to type *Adrian Taylor-Beaumont* into the search engine again.

She busied herself in the garden, made a vegetable casserole for dinner and finished unpacking the remains of the boxes, which she tore so that they could be stored flat, and put into the shed. It was only then that she realised with a start that she hadn't seen the dogs since lunchtime.

For a second she felt a heart wrenching feeling of panic but she quickly discovered Rollins curled up on one of the garden chairs, fast asleep. Searching revealed no sign of Aymes though. Finally, she found him curled up on a patch of grass under a bush near the shed. He looked up at her very trustingly, but did not want to emerge. There was definitely something that was bothering him. She made a mental note to ask Janette if there was a local vet. If he carried on like this, he might need something to calm him.

That evening, as she was sitting in the garden, watching the bats swoop, she heard the gate open and close and when she looked, there was Adrian standing just inside it. He was in his uniform again and was carrying his cap in his hand. He greeted her in the same slightly distant manner, but sat down in his customary chair. As always he refused her offer of refreshment. This time however, feeling the need for something to boost her, Magda went in to pour herself a glass of wine. She had resigned herself to the fact that he might have left when she came out but was still sitting there. There was a calmness about him this time that she had not noticed previously and to her it signified that he was beginning to feel comfortable in her presence. Which made her extraordinarily and inexplicably happy.

This time they talked far into the evening, Magda hardly noticing the temperature dropping as the night descended, despite wearing only a strappy, cotton sundress. She was mesmerised by Adrian's voice. He spoke in such a gentle and rather old-fashioned manner, and she found him fascinating. There was something of Dennis in him she began to realise as he talked, despite the fact that his accent was upper class English whereas Dennis had had the softly lilting Southern Irish inflection common to his place of birth. When, eventually she glanced at her watch, she was startled to find it was almost one in the morning.

Not wanting to break the spell, she said nothing of the time to Adrian, but almost as if he were in tune with her, he got up to leave. She wanted to detain him, to put her hand on his arm and beg him not to leave: to invite him inside and…yes, into her bed. The feeling was so strong it quite took her breath away. It was like being poised on the edge of a diving board, when you knew the drop would feel stomach churning and perilous when you left the board's security, and that the water would feel chest-numbingly cold when reached. However, she wanted it, wanted him more than anything she had ever wanted in her life. Looking up at him, she felt as if he could read her mind and that he must take her hand and lead her inside but it didn't happen and with a brief 'Goodnight' he was gone, leaving Magda stunned and speechless in his wake.

Despite the coolness of the night air, she sat there without moving for ages, shocked by both her thoughts and feelings, as well as by the abrupt way in which Adrian had left. She shivered. If he had indeed been able to read her thoughts, they must have repelled him for him to go like that.

She became aware of Rollins' wet nose nuzzling into her hand. Absentmindedly she stroked his silky head. From out of his place under the bush, Aymes emerged timorously, looking around him in the manner that told her he had in fact, been sleeping there almost all day.

She went in, taking her empty glass, which despite the late hour, she refilled. She gave the dogs their night time biscuit apiece and turning off the kitchen light, took the wine up to bed with her.

Chapter Ten

MAGDA was awoken rudely the next morning by the sound of extremely loud music emanating from the Griffiths' cottage. The thump, thump of the bass line seemed to reverberate right through her and Magda grimaced as she thought of Max and how right he might be about her wishing she had accompanied him to get away from here. Mentally she made a note to ask Gemma when they were actually leaving. She might also drop a hint that this volume of music in the quiet solitude of the cul-de-sac was simply not acceptable. Rather wearily she got out of bed and went downstairs. She let the dogs out and began to make coffee.

The phone rang and it was Janette asking her about the job. She told her that she had sent in the application and Janette was delighted.

'Just to let you know too, that I'm going away for a few days, back to see Rose. Not driven out by the horrendous Justin, and his taste in music, I promise, but rather something planned a few days ago.'

Magda told Janette she would miss her and that she was lucky to be escaping. As she hung up, Magda realised that apart from the Griffiths, she would be the only person left in the cottages. A feeling of loneliness descended so sharply it almost took her breath away.

Rousing herself she reminded herself how lucky she was with neighbours, who were now her friends. She poured a strong cup of coffee, and sliced a banana which she ate with some probiotic yoghurt for breakfast. After eating, she turned on her computer which pinged to indicate an incoming email. It was an acknowledgement of her application for the job. *No going back now*, she thought.

She went upstairs to have a shower and got dressed. Once again it was very hot and she made a mental note to go and water Max's garden and plants.

Just as she was about to go and see if Gemma wanted to go for a walk, the phone rang. It was Beth and they settled down to a long conversation concluding only when Beth asked if she would like to meet up and they arranged for Magda to visit with her dogs on the following Wednesday.

'You can stay the night if you'd like to?' Beth said.

'Actually, I would, very much, if that's all right?'

'Most certainly. It will give me longer to spoil those two lovely little boys and we can have a nice dinner together. I look forward to it.'

When she disconnected Magda found that she also was looking forward to it; very much. Beth was one of the only connections she had now with Dennis. She had heard nothing from his mother or sister, despite having sent them a card with her new address and telephone number.

Feeling invigorated by the thought of a little break away, she took the leads, clipped them on and went to knock at Gemma's cottage. Ray Griffiths answered and she could see immediately that he was not in the best of moods. The music had ceased about fifteen minutes previously and Magda could see Justin at the window as usual, leaning out and smoking. Ray did not invite her in but turned without a word and shouted for Gemma. Gemma came bounding down the stairs but was still in her night things. She looked suspiciously like she had been crying, her eyes red and watery.

'Hello Gemma, just wondered if you wanted to come for a walk with the dogs?'

Gemma sniffed and wiped her nose with the back of her hand. 'Sorry I can't. My mum's not well,' was all she said before she turned and went back upstairs.

Ray managed a smile which was more like a grimace, before shutting the door almost in her face. Magda wondered what was going on and whether she should alert someone.

She knocked hopefully on Janette's door, wanting to unload some of this onto the social worker's competent shoulders, but there was no answer, and then she noticed the lack of Janette's car in the drive. *Of course*, she remembered, *Janette's away*.

Magda and the dogs walked on to the river. Once again, the lovely views over the flat, still countryside cheered her and her thoughts moved back to Adrian, who was never far from her mind these days.

The two dogs splashed about in the water as Magda threw a rubber ball she had brought for them. Aymes, despite being the more timid of the two, was fearless about going in to fetch it and bring it back.

Tired, Magda lay down on the grass and closed her eyes for a moment. The dream was there immediately, pulsing behind her eyes, overwhelming her senses.

This time it was slightly different. She became aware of an orange ball of fire which seemed to be coming for her out of nowhere. Looking harder, she realised that a plane had come down and was on fire in one of the fields. Cautiously she approached and as she got nearer felt the scorching, blistering heat coming at her like a wall. There were men running around shouting. She knew, without being told that someone was still in the plane.

She began to run, ignoring the searing heat which seemed to burn right through her clothes and skin. I'll have blisters was all she thought as she almost reached the burning plane.

She was jolted awake by a cold wet nose and a tongue licking at her face. At first, she was afraid to open her eyes for fear of seeing someone burnt alive from the plane. The insistent licking persisted and when she finally found the courage to open her eyes, she found it was Rollins intent on waking her. Aymes was hiding under a nearby bush.

Warily Magda looked around for the plane, but there was nothing. Just the gentle rolling countryside, the ripened fields and the sluggish brown river rolling along on toward the sea. No plane, nothing burning, in fact nothing at all out of the ordinary.

Something, though, had obviously frightened Aymes and Magda wondered whether she had screamed aloud as she dreamt. Her heart was beating rapidly and she felt nauseous as she tried to get up. This time the dream had been horrible beyond belief. She knew, without a doubt that someone had burned either in the plane or on the ground. From childhood she had felt an irrational fear of fire. She remembered reading one of a series of books that she had loved about a boarding school. In this one there had been a fire and Magda had abandoned the book without finishing it, hiding it in the airing cupboard in the hall.

Finally, she managed to get onto her feet without throwing up and took some deep, soothing breaths before calling the dogs and attaching their leads. She remained shaky for the duration of the walk back. More than anything she wished Max was home so that she could avail herself of his cheerful, down to earth presence. She found, as she got nearer home, that she was actually dreading going back inside.

This is nonsense, she told herself firmly, as she walked up the path to the front door. Once inside, she sank down onto the settee in the kitchen and tried to steady her still rapidly beating heart. *It's nothing*, she told herself, *just a panic attack. Take deep breaths, in and out, and you'll be fine.*

She tried this for several minutes. Eventually, she felt strong enough to stand and go to fill the kettle to make a cup of tea. She took the tea into the lounge and switched on the television. She needed something mindless to ground her back into the real world, a world away from the dream and the burning.

What she found was a programme about selling antiques and she sat there mesmerised like a zombie, as gradually normality returned. After about an hour, and feeling as if her brain might turn to mush if she had to watch any more people ooing and aaahing over the value of treasured family heirlooms, she went back into the kitchen and fed the dogs. She made a sandwich for herself, poured a large glass of cold white wine and took them into the garden.

After lunch, she went over to Max's cottage and watered his indoor plants. Although she had been told it was a myth to wait for evening to water outdoor plants, she still held firmly to this adage and decided she would do both hers and Max's that evening. She got the hose out of the shed and attached it to the outside tap. It looked as if it might be long enough so that she could just reach over the fence into Max's garden.

The key to keeping all the nastiness of the dream at bay, she decided, was to keep busy. She vacuumed the downstairs, dusted the lounge and then cleaned the sink in the kitchen. Pleased with herself and now feeling more relaxed, she decided to give the dogs one more run for the day. They were thrilled and accompanied her gleefully. She avoided the river this time and walked a different way, finding herself in a small wood.

At first it felt a bit eerie, with the evening sun dappling through the overhanging tree branches, but soon she became accustomed to it. She could hear a woodpecker burring away in the distance and the sounds of other birds. She wished she was able to recognise their calls but couldn't. *I'll have to get a book* she thought. Then she laughed quietly to herself. *I'm turning into a real country bumpkin. I wonder what Dennis would think?*

Surprised, she realised this was the first time she had felt able to think about him without wanting to dissolve into tears. She wasn't sure if she liked this or not. She knew without doubt, that she never wanted to forget him but felt sadly, that with time, this was inevitable. *I'll never forget him totally*, she mused but knew that that memory would somehow fade with the distance of time. She wished his family liked her more. That way she could have been close to them.

The dogs were burrowing excitedly near a tree and she was concerned for a minute that they might have found an animal. Rollins emerged carrying what looked like a piece of cloth in his mouth. Magda shouted for him to put it down. It looked filthy, as if it had lain there for years. He was reluctant to release his treasure, so she bent down and took it gently from his mouth. As she held it, a strange feeling came over her and she rushed to shake the nasty thing free from her hands.

'Come on boys, let's go back,' she called to the dogs, and they came back over to her straightaway. She was relieved to see that Rollins had not gone back to retrieve the cloth. However, Aymes was shivering again beside her and looking spooked.

'It's okay little boy. It's probably the shady trees making you feel strange.' As she spoke, she became aware that she was voicing this as much for her own sake as the nervous little dog's. She was relieved when they reached the edge of the wood and could emerge into the sinking daylight again.

Once home, she began to prepare her evening meal. She took a portion of casserole she had made and frozen a few days ago and put it into the oven to heat. Suddenly for no reason, she thought of the generator, idling there in the shed and the thought alarmed her. It was okay to have it when Max was around and would know what to do with it but she suddenly disliked the idea of its presence and had absolutely no idea why she felt that way. She found her current book and settled outside to read until the dinner was ready.

The oven timer alerted her to the readiness of her evening meal, so she placed the bookmark Dennis had given her, in her book and walked back inside. There was no sign of either of the dogs but the meal was delicious and she was quite hungry. She had a glass of cold white wine with it and some focaccia bread she had defrosted. She finished with a nectarine and a cup of black coffee.

She went back to the book for a while and then got up and went outside to water the gardens. When this was done, she went in and rang an old friend, feeling she was becoming too preoccupied and isolated and needing to do something about it. They chatted for a while before Magda hung up, poured another glass of wine and took this out into the now darkening garden.

Of course, he was there. She had known or sensed he would be. It was as if all day had been leading up to this moment.

As before they chatted easily together, despite his rather stuffy, upright demeanour. He talked again about his family and their home in Wiltshire, painting such a verbal picture that Magda felt as if she were there, among the softly rolling hills around his childhood home. She told him about her life in London, about Dennis and about her decision to move to the cottage.

'I'm so glad I did.' She told him somewhat archly, hoping he might pick up on the nuance and subtext. He did not however, which she found disappointing. Instead after about ten more minutes, he rose and said he had to be going.

Magda felt an intense sense of disappointment as she accompanied him down the path to the gate. She wanted to ask when he might return, but something, pride she guessed, stopped her and she simply bade him goodnight.

A few minutes later the loud music started up again and she saw Gemma running towards her. 'Hi Magda, how are you? Sorry about dad. Can we go for a walk together tomorrow? I've missed the dogs. How are they? Oh, and I've missed you too.' This last was said with the nonchalance of a teenager, slightly embarrassed, but feeling she ought.

'Yes of course, they'll love it. Don't worry about your dad. Is everything alright now at home?'

Gemma could not look her in the eye, but shrugged her shoulders as if to say, 'You know how it is.'

Magda hesitated. She wanted to say something about the music but then decided against it and let the moment pass. Gemma had enough to deal with she reasoned as she turned to go back inside.

Chapter Eleven

TO her considerable relief that night proved dreamless. She awoke as usual to the sun pouring in and realised she hadn't closed the curtains the night before.

Both dogs were raring to start the day, so they all went downstairs and she let them into the garden, as she filled the kettle. Idly she picked up her book and found that the bookmark was no longer there, marking her place. She felt a feeling of panic as she hunted under the table. She remembered vividly placing it in the book the day before. It was one of the first things Dennis had given her. It was a corny gift she knew, a soft brown stiff body with a dog's head at the top. The long part went into the book, leaving just the head peering out. She had loved it as she loved him, she remembered. A few minutes hunting around revealed nothing, so she abandoned the search in favour of making coffee and giving the dogs their breakfast.

Just then the telephone rang and she went to answer it. It was Beth, sounding very upset, as she told Magda they would need to postpone their get together as an old and very dear friend had just been hospitalised with a heart attack and Beth was going down to Hampshire to look after her, when she was released from hospital.

'It's a mild one they say, but I need to go down. I'm so sorry. I was really looking forward to seeing you again. You do understand, don't you my dear?'

Assuring her friend that of course she did, Magda said her goodbyes and told Beth she was there for her, if she needed to ring her anytime.

'So, no trip to London for us,' she told the dogs, who were watching her in hope of maybe something more to eat.

After breakfast and a shower, she set about systematically looking for the bookmark. Half an hour or so later, she had to admit defeat. She had looked everywhere and had not found it. She found herself crying as she searched under the seats in the garden. Just then Gemma arrived, so Magda forced herself to cheer up and they set off together for their walk, Gemma proudly holding on to the dogs' leads.

They had a good walk but Gemma told Magda that sadly they were leaving sooner than planned. 'Dad wants to go home for some boring dinner thing that he and mum have been invited to. Then there's some week long course thingy for Jus to go on; Outward-Bound or something equally lame. Jus is pissed off too as he doesn't want to go. So, tomorrow might be our last chance for a walk.'

Magda was saddened too, seeing that Gemma had tears in her eyes, which she hastily wiped away with her arm.

'That's a shame, but then you've got the Maldives, which I'm sure will be lovely. Then you never know, you might come back here before you go back to school.'

Magda wondered if the sudden departure might have something to do with Ray hitting his wife and the fear that Magda had found out. However, she said nothing, just reiterating what she had told Gemma before, that she could ring her whenever she needed to and smiling to herself imagining the languid Justin on an Outward-Bound course.

Gemma went back home quite cheerily when they got back, agreeing that they would walk again the following morning.

Magda went inside feeling rather down and lonely. She missed both Max and Janette and was, she had to admit, finding the cottage a little spooky lately, with the dreams and everything else.

She hoped Adrian might return that evening and wondered if she dare invited him to come for a meal with her at some point. She vowed she would at least ask him for his telephone number. They had shared a few evenings together now, so surely that would not seem too forward? Somehow though, Magda felt he might view it so. Magda herself was not very worldly. She had had a couple of boyfriends before meeting Dennis, but nothing very serious. Dennis in his quiet way had swept her off her feet and she had known almost immediately that he was the one for her. He had confessed that he had felt the same after only their first date. If she was honest, she admitted to herself, she was beginning to feel the same way about Adrian, although they had not even done so much as kiss. She had to admit that feeling this way was very unsettling.

She spent a busy day in the garden and also went across again to check on Max's plants. She was surprised at how much she was missing him. She harboured no romantic feelings towards him, but she enjoyed his company immensely. She took the dogs for another short walk that afternoon and when she got back, was surprised to find that for the first time in ages, it had clouded over and looked as if rain might threaten. This made her feel anxious as she wouldn't be able to sit in the garden, waiting for Adrian if it poured with rain. She didn't know why, but she couldn't imagine him doing something as ordinary as knocking on the door and coming to sit inside. He seemed as if he always just materialised out of the blue.

Her fears, however, were short lived as about an hour and a half later the sun emerged as bright and warm as ever. This really was the most unusual spell of good weather for years. Magda vaguely remembered another hot summer when she had been growing up but could not for the life of her remember which year that had been. She thought she had been at secondary school so put it in the early eighties. She made herself a meal, fed the dogs and took her food outside to eat. The evening was very still again, hardly a breath of wind. She looked over at Max's shrubs and noted thankfully that they were not drooping or wilting.

The evening descended into night and still she waited for Adrian. At around ten-thirty, she realised with a real stab of disappointment that he was not going to come. As she got up to go inside, she felt tears well up in her eyes and chided herself for being stupid. She knew she was lonely, grieving and unsettled at this time and this had to be why she was becoming fixated on this man. She noted with a start too that he never now mentioned Maria.

Weary and feeling very sad she went up to bed. Both dogs had already gone up and were lying on her bed. She cuddled them to her and was thankful to Beth for bringing these two little warm, loving bodies into her life. She fell asleep almost immediately and began to dream.

It was the same as the dream she had had by the river. The burning, the urgency, the woman running along beside her in the long white nightgown. This time however, and she didn't know why, she felt that Adrian was in the dream with her. She was afraid for him, for his safety and felt powerless to stop whatever was going to happen. All she knew, deep down, was that whatever it was, it was a tragedy; something that could not be resolved. She could feel the heat, smell the burning, hear the shouting, yet could do nothing, nothing but run alongside this ethereal lady who seemingly needed her help.

She did not know what had awakened her, but suddenly she was conscious and sitting bold upright in her bed, with perspiration and tears streaming down her face. She thought, just like before, that she caught a glimpse of white by the window but when she wiped the tears from her eyes, it had disappeared, if it had ever been there. Her heart was pounding and she felt as if she might throw up.

Trying to calm herself with deep breaths, she lay back down in bed. The room was spinning as if she had drunk too much alcohol. Closer investigation revealed that only Rollins was now on the bed and that once again there was no sign of Aymes. Magda wondered for a split second if in fact she was going mad.

She was unable to settle so went downstairs to make a cup of tea. Rollins padded down with her and she opened the door to let him out. He ran out and lifted his leg on the nearest bush, before rushing back inside. Magda found herself looking out through the back door for Adrian, but the garden remained empty, silent and still.

Aymes appeared just as Magda had made her tea. He went to the back door, but when she opened it was hesitant about going outside until the need to relieve himself won out and he went over and lifted his leg on the same bush that had been watered a few minutes earlier by Rollins. When he returned to the kitchen, Magda gave them both a milky bone biscuit and then took her tea outside.

The night was very warm still. The darkness was almost total as there was just the slimmest of crescent moons. She sought the star that she felt was Dennis and took comfort when she found it. It twinkled brightly and this gave her some hope and solace.

'I miss you,' she whispered, meaning it.

Then as so often now, her mind went to Adrian and she felt such an intense pang of disloyalty it hurt. It was too soon. Wearily she went back inside. A glance at the clock on the kitchen wall told her it was ten minutes past three. She found her book and took it up to bed. She felt too wired to sleep and so opened it, remembering as she did so, that she had been unable to find the bookmark. *I won't think about that*, she told herself and willed herself to concentrate on the written words of the page.

It was no good, she couldn't so she fumbled around for the remote control and turned on the television. Turning to the *True Movies* channel, she was soon immersed in a film about two babies who had been switched at birth. This helped take her mind of herself and all her emotions and she must have dozed as next thing she knew it was daylight. She was half propped up on her pillows, feeling slightly uncomfortable with a crick in her neck. The clock showed six twenty and the television continued to play.

Stiffly, she climbed out of bed and went to switch it off. Both dogs got up and nuzzled at her legs. She felt stiff and sore but went downstairs and opened the door for the dogs. She thought for a second that there was someone in Max's garden but closer inspection revealed nothing there. Suddenly she didn't feel as if she could cope with Gemma walking with her today. She felt so sad and tired. She decided she would trust Gemma with her beloved dogs to walk on her own. The girl undoubtedly loved them and seemed very sensible for her age.

This plan was to be foiled however. After breakfast Gemma arrived with

Justin in tow.

'Hi Magda, is it okay if Jus comes with us? I've been telling him about you and the dogs and he wants to come.'

Magda really did not feel like the company of the boy who seemed so arrogant and played the dreadfully loud music, but good manners on her part left her no choice but to agree to the unwelcome request.

She found the leads and they set off. At first Justin seemed supercilious as Gemma chatted away about the coming week but when she mentioned the Outward-Bound course, Justin scowled and swore and said that he didn't want to go. He looked young and vulnerable for a split second and Magda felt herself warm towards him. He like Gemma, was simply a victim of his family, or rather his father.

'I don't know much about them, but it might be fun. Will you be in a hostel or something? You never know, there could be girls!'

This actually elicited a smile from him and as if the floodgates had opened he began to talk about his and Gemma's life with their father. By now they had reached the garage and shop and Justin insisted on going in and buying ice creams for them all.

'Wow, I've never heard Jus talk like that before!' Gemma exclaimed as he walked towards the shop. 'He never tells anyone about Dad.'

Magda didn't know whether to be alarmed or flattered by this. She wished she was in a position to help these two victims of what was looking more and more like domestic abuse.

Justin returned with the ice creams and when Magda thanked him, he smiled. He was very handsome when he wasn't scowling Magda realised, rather like his sister with fair, typically English good looks.

They wandered along in silence while they ate their ice creams. Gemma asked if she could give some to the dogs and when Magda agreed, both she and Justin shared their cones. Justin then suggested they let them off the leads as they had reached the river. He marvelled at their speed and laughed at their antics in the river when Gemma threw in their ball. 'Gem said this was fun. I laughed at her at first, but it is. Thank you.'

Magda told him he was welcome and they sat on the bank together in a rather comfortable silence, watching Gemma throw the ball time and again, with consummate patience. After half an hour or so and when Gemma said her arm was hanging off they set out for home. The encounter had lifted Magda spirits no end.

Gemma hugged her goodbye and the dogs too when they reached home.

Magda assured her that they would all be here when the Griffiths returned next, and then out of the blue Justin gave her a slightly wooden hug. Wishing them both well for their journey home, their following week and their imminent holiday, Magda waved them goodbye as she walked through her gate. *Who would have thought it?* she marvelled as she walked up the path.

In the warm sunshine the cottage seemed welcoming and serene, unlike the previous night. She put a bowl of fresh water down for the dogs, who began lapping furiously. She made herself a cup of tea, deeming it too early in the day for wine, although she was crying out for a glass. She drank the tea, watered her own indoor plants and then made herself a salad with cheese for lunch. This time she ate inside watched closely by the dogs, ever hopeful of something dropped on the floor. The afternoon seemed to stretch ahead. She felt tired and lazy after her broken night and considered an afternoon nap, before dismissing this as self-indulgent. Her mother's voice floated into her mind. 'If you sleep now, you won't sleep tonight.' This brought a smile to her face.

There was another storm that night. Not quite as vicious as the last one she had experienced but with a bit of thunder and lightning and the type of torrential rain that seems to accompany thunder storms. This one was short-lived and soon over and the electricity supply held, much to her relief. There were no dreams either when she did finally fall asleep.

On waking and getting up she went out to examine the garden for damage and found nothing too bad. It was yet another hot, sweltering morning, even at this early hour. The storm had done nothing to clear the air.

When she got downstairs she found a large brown envelope on the mat by the front door, with *Cambridgeshire NHS Trust* stamped on it. *The job*, she thought excitedly, noting that the envelope was large and thick and that rejections usually came in a slimmer form. Upon opening it, she found that it contained an interview invitation, further details of the post, a health questionnaire for her to complete and best of all; directions how to get there. The interview was for the following week and she was asked to call to confirm attendance.

She waited until nine-thirty before ringing as she didn't wish to appear desperate. She was surprised at how excited the prospect felt and realised anew how much she had missed working at something she had in the past enjoyed so much. Looking through the paperwork she saw there was nothing she would be unable to handle and the fact that it was for only eighteen hours each week meant she wouldn't have to leave the dogs alone for long every day. She thought how pleased Dennis would have been if she were in fact to be offered the job.

After she had telephoned and spoken to someone who sounded lovely, and told her they were pleased she could attend, she got the dogs ready for their walk.

At the shop Linda greeted her like an old friend, and took a bowl of water out for the dogs. She reminded Magda that Margaret had thoroughly enjoyed talking to her and was hoping she would return if she had time.

Down by the river she was amazed and startled to see a Kingfisher darting among the reeds. It was so beautiful with its vibrant colour it quite took her breath away. *I'm so lucky to live here*, she thought, *and soon I might have a job too.* The future seemed suddenly hopeful.

When she got back, she looked for Huntingdon and programmed the address into her satnav. She completed the health questionnaire, placed it into the return envelope they had provided and then realised she had not noticed a post box anywhere since coming to live in the cottage. *There's got to be one somewhere* she thought, and once again, wished that Max was home so that she could have asked him. Thus reminded about his plants, she went next door to water them.

As she came out, she saw the Griffiths piling into their people carrier, about to set off for home. Both Gemma and Justin waved to her, calling their loud goodbyes out of the window as they drove off. She hoped that their holiday would bring some happiness to Gemma and even to Emily as that seemed to be a commodity in short supply for them both.

She spent a lazy day in the garden reading before making herself yet another casserole, which she placed in the oven. She got the dogs leads, the letter and set off in search of a post box, whilst the meal was cooking. She found one at the garage, which she had never noticed before, and put the letter inside. Jim at the cash till gave her a friendly wave which she returned before walking back along the river bank. The health questionnaire had made her realise that she was not registered with a doctor in the area. It had asked for her GP and she had listed the one from Highgate in case they wanted to check up that she had been honest in her answers. Again, she had no idea where the nearest one might be was but guessed it would be in Ramsey. She made a mental note to look it up on the computer and then drive in during the week to register. *I'll need a vet too for the dogs, and a dentist,* she thought.

As usual she took her evening meal outside. The dogs had been fed and she poured herself a glass of wine. The garden was beginning to look lovely and now far better cared for than when she had first arrived. She stayed outside as first evening and then night fell. *I am not waiting for Adrian*, she told herself, but knew in her heart that this was untrue.

At just before ten, when she was thinking of going inside, the gate creaked open and in he walked. In uniform he looked strikingly handsome. Her heart missed a beat and she felt a lump form in her throat. *I want to kiss him* she thought, before banishing the thought as quickly as it had arrived.

Her hands were trembling as he approached and sat down.

'I hope you don't mind my calling so late?' were his first words.

'No, not at all. You are very welcome. Can I get you anything? A cup of tea, glass of wine?'

Slowly he shook his head. 'It's a beautiful evening isn't it?' He sounded a little sad.

'Very. I cannot believe what a lovely summer we're having.'

Magda found the conversation stilted. She wanted to break through the barriers she felt were in place, but seemed powerless to do so.

They continued to chat about the weather for a while and then Adrian began to talk about previous years and harvests in the Wiltshire countryside where he had grown up. 'We used to go and help the farmer. It was quite a day for us.'

Magda asked who he meant and he explained it was his brother and sister. He spoke then about the Shire horses the farmers used and this made her quite surprised as it sounded very outmoded. *Maybe it's one of those organic back to rural nature types of farm*, she thought as he went on describing the process and the Harvest Supper which always followed. *He has a brother and sister*, she found herself thinking and this made him seem more human somehow. She was aware that she wanted to question him avidly; to find out everything about him. Like someone starving for sustenance she was hungry to know this enigmatic man better. She did not recall ever having felt this way before, even with Dennis. With Dennis they had shared everything easily; their growing up years, university experiences, likes, dislikes, everything. Adrian was far more reticent, making Magda feel intrusive, almost like a voyeur. It was not a comfortable feeling.

As the night descended and it grew darker they talked on. Magda told him about Dennis; things she had shared with no one before. He talked about his family and the air force. It was one in the morning before he got up to leave.

He will kiss me now, this time I know he will Magda thought as they rose together but he did nothing of the sort. Simply taking his cap from the table, he smiled, bade her goodnight and with a wave somewhat in the manner of Max, whenever he left, he took his leave.

He just thinks of me as a friend, nothing more. Magda chided herself and was amazed to discover how crushed she felt by this. Unable to shake the feeling of such intense disappointment, she was unable to get to sleep. She turned the television on, then off again, irritated by what it had to offer. She took her book from the bedside table but when she had read the same few lines over and over without taking in a word, she abandoned that in favour of going downstairs for a glass of brandy. The more she tried to will herself to sleep, the harder it became. Their conversation together played over and over in her head, taunting her with its glimpses of intimacy. Finally, exhausted, at about four-thirty she fell into an uneasy sleep. Luckily for her there were no dreams, but even so, when she woke she felt exhausted from such a broken night.

As she went about her daily tasks all she kept thinking was *why doesn't he find me attractive?* She kept looking at herself in the bathroom mirror every time she went in there. She studied her face from all angles and then tried pinning her hair up, then taking it down and pinning some of it back. It was thick, dark, lustrous, wavy hair. She had been told that her hair and her eyes were her best features. Dennis had loved her hair, had loved nothing better than running his hands through it, gripping it tightly when they made love. She knew she was ordinary, but had always thought herself passable. Now she wished she were a beauty and then he would be bound to fall in love with her. She was not fat; she was of average height and she had no apparent disfigurements but still he didn't seem to want her. She wished she could see a photograph of Maria, to see what she might be up against although these days he never mentioned her. *Was he pining for her? Was he wishing Magda was Maria? Was he just using her as someone to help him get over the loss of her?*

Magda wished Max was home so that she could talk to him. Get a man's perspective. For such a good therapist, she felt hopeless in the onslaught of her feelings. *What would you tell a client in the same situation?* she asked herself, but was unable to find an answer. Was she going mad after all? Or was this grief striking anew? She had no answers. That evening she decided against sitting outside. *I won't sit there and wait for him*, she thought as she set the kitchen table with a plate knife and fork. *I'm just going to carry on as normal and do everything I need to.* She ate her meal with her book propped up in front of her and actually managed to concentrate on what she was reading. Later on she went online and searched for a doctor's surgery, a dentist and a vet, making a note of the telephone numbers. Her fingers hesitated for a moment over *Google*, but she made herself ignore the urge to put in his name once again. Later that evening she went to bed, where she slept the sleep of the dead.

Chapter Twelve

AS her interview came nearer, she began to get nervous. On the actual day, she rose early and was spurred on by finding a postcard from Max waiting for her on the door mat. Corsica looked absolutely gorgeous, all blue sea and sun. For an instant she regretted not taking him up on his offer.

She did all her routine tasks; fed the dogs, had breakfast and then took them for a walk. Her interview was at two. She gave herself plenty of time to get there and was in fact, nearly an hour early.

She parked her car at *Sainsbury's* and went inside to have a coffee and a sandwich in their little café. She walked to the hospital. The day, once again, was a warm one and she had decided on a beige linen dress with a lacy pale mauve bolero over the top. She had wondered if she should wear shoes instead of sandals, but it was so hot she had decided on a smart pair of leather ones Dennis had bought for her when they were on holiday in Italy.

She gave her name at reception and was given a plastic visitor's badge to pin on. After about ten minutes a very pretty, smiling young lady came down and walked over to her.

'Hi, are you Magda?' Magda nodded. 'I'm Jenny, the PTS secretary.'

'Nice to meet you.' Magda offered her hand to be shaken. She knew from her old job that PTS stood for Psychological Therapy Service. She remembered too how invaluable Julia the departmental secretary had been at her previous workplace.

The interview seemed to go well. The head of department, together with the service team leader and service manager comprised the panel and they went out of their way to put Magda at her ease. After some tricky questions, which she managed to answer succinctly enough, they began to chat about the department which they impressed upon her was a friendly and warm place to work. As she got up to leave, the head of department, a small, wiry man with horn-rimmed glasses gave her a warm smile, together with a slight nod as if to indicate that she was seen by him at least as being appointable. She left on a high and walked back to get her car.

On the journey home she listened to the radio, singing along to some of the songs she recognised. She felt good about the job and knew that if they offered it to her, she would accept. She knew too that she had spent too much time in the cottage alone and the result was her growing obsession with Adrian Taylor-Beaumont. A new job would give her something else on which to focus.

As she had hoped, they offered her the post the following day. She was absolutely thrilled, but then dismayed when they told her they did not want her to start for six weeks. They said it was because it was holiday time and that there would be nobody there to undertake the orientation process they used and that she also needed to be seen by Occupational Health for a blood test and to make sure her immunisations were all current. Despite that slight disappointment she readily accepted the job, telling herself that six weeks would pass quickly. The following day she registered with a doctor in Ramsey and completed a new patient' questionnaire. They were very nice at the surgery and said if she could wait twenty minutes the nurse would see her for her initial check-up. She did and the smiling nurse was lovely. Everything was fine and she pronounced Magda to be 'In excellent health.'

Next she walked to the dental surgery she had discovered online and registered there.

The last thing was the vet where she met a good looking South African who told her he would be delighted to meet Aymes and Rollins, should the need arise.

She left the town with a sense of achievement, popping in to a small supermarket to get some bread and milk before going back home.

She was thrilled to see Janette's car parked outside the cottage and when she had put away her shopping and let the dogs out, she cut a bunch of flowers from the garden, took a bottle of wine from the cupboard and walked to her friend's cottage. Janette was pleased to see her too and they hugged. She was delighted to hear about the job and insisted they open the bottle right away to celebrate, despite it being only midday. Then she showed Magda yet more photos of Rose, who was looking more human now that she had grown a little. She was indeed a very sweet little baby.

'Oh, by the way, I remembered that Mrs. Grigson's son, the one who inherited your cottage, found a whole lot of documents and things in the attic, when he cleared out. I know he's in Australia, but he might have kept some of them. Maybe they could shed some light on your Maria. I only thought of this while I was away. I remember he asked me if I wanted to see them or keep them. I wasn't that interested at the time, I confess, but wish now I had. I'll look out his address I'm sure I kept it. Then maybe you could write or email or something, see if he's still got them.'

Magda felt a frisson of excitement go through her at this. It was quickly followed by an intense feeling of anxiety that Mrs. Grigson's son might have destroyed them. In all honesty she couldn't imagine him carting them back to Australia with him. She thanked Janette though and said she would be very grateful for the contact details.

After they had finished the wine and the sandwiches Janette had insisted on making, she went home to be greeted in their usual exuberant fashion by her dogs and she decided to treat them to a walk.

Strangely enough the day had cooled considerably for the first time in ages so Magda found a light cardigan which she tied round her waist just in case she needed it later and they set off. She went to the river as usual and en-route spotted an elderly man wearing a cap and dungarees, doing something in one of the hedgerows. As she got nearer, he turned and raised the cap in a gesture of deference. He was elderly but had bright twinkling blue eyes.

'Afternoon,' he greeted her in a strong Cambridgeshire accent.

'Good afternoon.'

'Nice dogs, do they go rabbiting?'

Magda shook her head.

'Oh well, that kind of pastime seems to have disappeared these days. I'm just doing a bit of tidying up here. Nobody seems to take much notice of these hedgerows nowadays, not like years ago.'

He was obviously a talker so Magda let the dogs off the lead. They raced over to the man and he bent down and stroked them in turn, murmuring to them as he did so. Within seconds he had started a long conversation. It turned out that he still lived in a cottage over on the other side of the river. He told her he had been born there and never left. Magda began to feel excited. Maybe he would know about the airfield. Tentatively when there was a break in his outpourings, Magda took a deep breath and asked her question. She was aware that she was actually holding her breath awaiting his answer.

'Oh aye, the old airfield. Course I remember it. It was very exciting, having it here. I used to watch the planes all the time. They didn't all come back you know, them brave lads what took off.'

He fell silent for a moment or two, contemplating their fate. 'There were some trouble up here one time, something with a woman what was involved with one of they pilots. I never really knew what it was about. My old mum didn't want me knowing that's for sure. Then there was a fire, up at your little cottages, if I remember right. Terrible. They changed the name of the one got burnt. I remember 'cos they was all named for flowers and then one changed. Not sure what went on, but I remember the fire 'cos me and

Albert, he was me mate, we came out to watch the fire engine that night.' Suddenly he began to run out of steam and he paused, taking a large, extremely white handkerchief out of his pocket with which he began to mop his brow. 'Sorry lass, I were just rememberin' Albert. He joined up not long after, got killed in France, the silly bugger.' This seemed to have tired him and Magda hesitated before saying more.

'I live in the one called Hornbeams.'

'Really? Well that's the one, the one what had the fire. I know that 'cos Hornbeam be a tree and like I said, they was all called after flowers. I think one were Honeysuckle.' He named the cottage that was now Janette's.

Magda was so excited she could hardly breathe.

He looked at her for a moment as if he had forgotten she was there. 'Sorry lass, it just takes me back that's all. I live over the field and the other side of the river. If you ever feel like paying a visit on an old man, you'd be more than welcome. I better get on though now.' He indicated the bag of weeds he must have pulled from the hedgerow. There was no mistaking that he was indicating their conversation was over.

Despite her instincts screaming to push him for more information, Magda thanked him, promising that she would visit in the near future.

With another formal doff of his cap he bade her goodbye, returning with his secateurs to the hedgerow.

Magda walked on feeling exhilarated, mulling over what he had said. A fire, a woman, a pilot; *what if the woman had been Maria?* But then she couldn't have been. Adrian had expected to find her here, now. She would be in her eighties at the youngest if she had been around in the war. Maria could be her daughter though, or granddaughter. *My God*, she thought. *Am I getting nearer finding the truth?* She felt a frisson of concern though when she thought about the fire, and in her home too. She did her best to dismiss those fears as unfounded. It had been years ago. The cottage had been completely refurbished, the heating system and the wiring were all new. She thought thankfully about the certificates she had been given to this effect on purchase, now lodged with the deeds at the solicitor's in Highgate. *Just because there was a fire there all those years ago, doesn't mean there'll be one again.* What was that saying about lightening not striking the same place twice?

By now she had reached the river. She looked across to see if she could spot the old man's cottage, but was unable to do so. She panicked for a second, wondering if she had imagined what happened, but as she walked further down, she could just about make out the roof all but hidden by a large tree. *He DID exist*, and she breathed a sigh of relief. Somehow, she felt she might be getting near to solving her mystery.

Chapter Thirteen

AFTER the dogs had had a good run, and as the day was now becoming very much cooler, Magda turned towards home. She hoped the weather wasn't going to break entirely. She had loved the freedom of the hot weather, being able to sit outside all the time and to take the dogs for long walks. If it turned cold or started to rain, she would be limited with what she might do.

She acknowledged too, that Adrian might not turn up if the evenings were no longer warm. She sat outside again later as she ate her evening meal. It was chilly, but not unpleasant and well worth it if he should decide to turn up. The dogs however, had retired inside to their beds, not appreciating the drop in temperature.

The sound of the telephone had her running inside. It was Janette with Mrs. Grigson's grandson's email. Magda checked that it was a grandson and not a son as people kept telling her it was both.

'Oh hang on, no it is her son. It's just that Max always says grandson, I don't know why.' Janette laughed and then went on to say she had also received a postcard from their lively neighbour. Magda thanked her for the address, went into the study and composed a short, polite, but friendly email to Mr Dan Grigson. This done she logged off her computer and went back outside taking a glass of wine with her.

He didn't come.

When finally it got too cool for Magda to stay in the garden, she got up, sighing in defeat, went inside and got ready for bed.

The dream came again. Horrendous in its detail. She could smell the smoke, the fire and burning flesh. Everything around was in turmoil and there was shouting coming from all sides. The sense of danger was overwhelming and once again, she looked down at her bare feet running down the road, as fast as they could take her. 'Basta, basta,' she heard someone shouting beside her and there was the woman; the same cloudy black hair, the same intense eyes. Then in front of her was a familiar figure – Adrian! She called and ran after him, but he disappeared right in front of her eyes, leaving her with such an intense feeling of loss. Then she woke up.

She was shivering and crying, her tears pooling down onto the duvet. 'Come back to me,' she whispered without realising she was actually speaking the words aloud. Gradually she managed to pull herself together, enough to open her eyes and achieve a sitting position on the bed. She heard the patter of raindrops on the window and noticed that there was no visible moon. Feeling as if she had just run a marathon, she crawled out of bed and over to the window.

It was raining quite hard and visibility was poor, but she felt certain for a second or two that there had been a shape over by the garden gate, a white shape. *It must be a barn owl,* she reasoned, *but why would it be by the gate?*

She still felt disoriented from the dream. There was no sign of either of the dogs, but closer inspection revealed them both under the duvet. Magda shivered as she reached for her dressing gown. Pulling it on and tying it round her, she padded downstairs to the kitchen to make tea. Rollins followed and demanded to be let out. He was ages outside and came back soaking wet. He shook himself all over Magda and she smiled. She felt overwhelmingly grateful for the presence of the dogs.

Reluctant to go back to bed she went into the study to turn on the computer. She had no idea as to the time in Australia but checked her email just in case and sure enough Dan Grigson had sent a reply. It was a disappointing one, however, as he had indeed got rid of the papers. He told her he thought he might have one or two left that he had put in his suitcase as a kind of memento of his mother's home but he wasn't sure what he had done with them. He promised to look for them and if he found them would let her know. He finished by saying he hoped she was happy in the property and wishing her well. *So, no real leads there.* Stretching, she turned off the computer and went back into the kitchen. For a second or two she contemplated turning on the central heating as there was a decided chill in the air. That seemed an admission of defeat though so she just made her way back up to bed.

Sleep proved completely elusive and once again she found herself watching a *True Movie'* into the small hours of the morning.

It was gone ten when she woke the next morning. She could hear the rain on the windows and looked out onto a dreary sodden world. Rousing the two dogs who were snoozing under the duvet, she went downstairs. They rushed out quickly and raced back inside, demanding breakfast and looking crestfallen at the change in the weather. Magda fed them, made herself toast and coffee and went into the lounge. She turned on the gas fire and soon the room seemed warm and cheery. The fire looked like a wood burner, but was fake, of course. She was glad as she knew she would not have the patience to deal with logs or clearing a fireplace each time the fire was lit.

She stayed inside reading and then heard the paper land on the mat. The paper boy was always late lately due to it being the school holidays. She chuckled to herself thinking of Linda's comments about him last time she had gone to pay the bill. She poured more coffee and began to solve the cryptic crossword. She became absorbed as usual and was only roused when she saw the postman cross past the window. She heard the letter box and went out to find a large brown envelope on the mat. It contained the appointment time for occupational health and a draft contract for her new job, which was subject, it said, to passing the health check. She knew it would be fine and that her vaccinations were all up to date.

She returned to the crossword and didn't even bother to go and have a shower until around half past eleven. When she looked out of her bedroom window later, she was pleased to see that the day had lightened and the rain had almost stopped. It was not nearly as warm as it had been though. She hoped summer wasn't over, so early in August. She had some lunch and set off with the dogs for a walk.

The sun by now had become pleasantly warm, dispersing her concerns about summer's end. As she reached the river, she saw, much to her surprise and delight, Adrian sitting on a bench. Her heart began to race, and her palms sweat as she walked over to him. He seemed lost in thought, so gently she tapped him on the shoulder. As she did so she felt a shiver down her spine, something her mother used to describe as 'someone walking over my grave.' The sensation dispersed immediately when he turned to her and smiled, greeting her warmly.

She sat down next to him as the dogs leapt and played on the river bank. In the sky there was the faint arc of a rainbow. They sat there in companionable silence for a long while, Magda hoping, almost pleading, mentally that Adrian would touch her; take her hand, kiss her, or give her some other indication that he felt the way she was beginning to feel about him. He did not do so and gradually Magda found an acceptance of this and simply revelled in his presence.

He laughed about the antics of the dogs and they both chatted for a while; inconsequential things like the weather, and Magda told him of her earlier despair that the summer might be over. He smiled at this, looking intently into her eyes. She was mesmerised and held her breath, thinking, *now, now surely he's going to touch me*, but he did not.

They must have spent over an hour sitting together and Magda was reluctant to break the spell and leave, but soon the dogs began to whine and bark indicating that they were ready to move on. Eventually she had to give in to their demands, and rose to go.

Adrian continued to sit looking out at the river. She told him she was going and he smiled that breath-taking smile at her, telling her how nice it was to see her, and that he hoped they might meet again soon.

As she turned away he seemed once again to be lost in thought. *I'll have to make do with those words* she thought as she called the dogs and walked away.

There were no dreams that night and Magda, refreshed got up to go into Peterborough to do some more shopping. She settled the dogs with some chews, filled water bowls and put down clean blankets in their beds, got the car out, chose a CD to listen to and began the, now familiar drive to the city.

Once there she parked near the cathedral and walked around the shops, finding a covered market, where she bought some lovely fruit, some new bedding and some treats for the dogs. She spent a good forty minutes in *Waterstones*, before crossing the road to *Asda* where she got a trolley and stocked up for the coming weeks. The day had become hot again and she was thirsty so she put all her shopping in the car, and went in search of a café. She found one and had a drink and a sandwich before driving home. She experienced a feeling of satisfaction. She was starting to become independent again after all those years of marriage, where she and Dennis had done almost everything together. If someone had told her that within less than a year of his death she would have been living somewhere completely new and making a life for herself she would not have thought it possible. But here she was doing just that. And she had Beth to thank for it. Beth had found her the dogs and the dogs had found her dream home.

She was surprised to realise that she had not thought about Adrian once since arriving in the city. *I must do this*, she told herself, *keep busy; fill my days. It's no good mooning over someone who clearly wants only to be friends*. The drive home was pleasant as she listened to Leonard Cohen, an old CD which had belonged to Dennis. With each song she remembered things about her husband and was surprised that the memories did not hurt quite as much as they had. She was moving on, moving forward and knew, in her heart of hearts that this was what Dennis would have wanted for her. In fact, it was almost as if his voice was whispering into her ear; 'I want you to be happy.'

'I am, Dennis,' she told him aloud and then smiled at herself for doing so.

Once home she unloaded the car and went in to be greeted rapturously by the dogs. She let them into the garden whilst she prepared their food. They ate with relish as always before going back outside and settling down together under a bush. They loved nothing more than lying cuddled together, just as they had done in the kennels when she and Beth had gone to find them. She made a mental note to telephone her friend to see if she was back and ask how Beth's convalescing friend was.

She felt very blessed. She made a cup of tea and took it outside with her book, to sit and read in the sun. The sun was now as hot as ever so the cooler, rainy weather had to have been a blip. She adjusted the recliner chair so that it went back and she lay there soaking up the sun.

She must have dozed because the next thing she knew, she was right inside a dream once again. This time there was no burning, no danger - just a woman and a man walking hand in hand along the river bank. They had their backs to her, but she could see them in clear detail. The woman was wearing a bright red dress which looked like it came from the nineteen thirties or forties calf-length and with square, padded shoulders. She had long luxuriant black hair reaching right down her back to her waist. She was wearing white high heeled shoes and her dress was cinched in at the waist with a broad white belt. The man was in uniform, the grey blue of the air force. His hair was military short and fair. Magda knew without being told that the woman was Maria. She watched as the couple meandered along hand in hand, before stopping for the man to bend and kiss the woman passionately for several seconds. It was a charming scene and it made Magda feel sad and yet, at the same time, hopeful. There was no mistaking that these two cared for each other greatly. They continued on their walk, keeping in step with each other as if they walked this way together all the time. Magda thought it must be spring as there were daffodils growing along the river bank and the trees were in bud rather than wearing the full-grown leaves of summertime. The scene was peaceful and tranquil unlike that of the previous dreams. She found she was holding her breath and silently willing them to turn around so that she could see their faces. Just as she thought they were about to, she woke up.

It took her a few seconds to re-orientate herself. Gradually she became aware that she felt calm and peaceful, not with the pounding heart and sweat drenched palms of before. This time she wished she could go back to revisit what she had just witnessed. It had been so incredibly beautiful. What she had seen was two people deeply in love taking a walk together. It made her think of Dennis and herself when they had first begun to date. That feeling as you walk through life that you are the only two people in the world who matter, and that around you everything is benign and wonderful.

She only realised then that what had woken her was Janette, standing over her.

'Hey Sleeping Beauty sorry to disturb you, but this was delivered while you were out.' Janette was holding a small package in her hands. 'The postman didn't think it would fit in the letter box and asked if I would take it in for you.'

Magda thanked her and asked if she'd like a cup of tea.

'Sorry, can't stop I just popped home to get something. I'm on duty today, so might be home late. Drink at the weekend instead?'

'Oh yes, lovely, I'll hold you to that and thanks for this.'

Magda relieved Janette of the package, which she saw bore an Australian postmark and stamps. She felt reluctant to open it and didn't know why. Eventually she took it inside, laid it on the kitchen table and poured herself a glass of wine. She took the wine and the parcel into the lounge and tore it open.

There was a short note attached to some very elderly and yellowed newspaper clippings. The note was from Mrs. Grigson's son. 'I hope you find the enclosed interesting and you don't need to return them.'

She looked at the first one. The headline read *Cottage fire is arson* and was dated July 1942. It stated that the police investigation into the recent fire at Lavender Cottage in the village near Ramsey showed that it was started deliberately, it was thought by someone putting a burning rag through the letterbox. *The sole inhabitant of the cottage, a Miss Maria Colleano was alone when this happened and subsequently died of smoke inhalation and burns. It was believed that Miss Colleano had foreign relatives in but none in England. The case remains open.*

Oh my God thought Magda, *this has to be Maria, Adrian's Maria.*

The next article was just a short piece detailing the fact that repairs were underway at the cottage where a fire had broken out the previous month.

The third cutting was a tribute to air force personnel killed in action. Reading down the list, Magda found a familiar name, Squadron Leader Adrian Taylor-Beaumont.

Magda could make no sense of this at all. Adrian was very much alive and far too young to have been in the Second World War. He was forty if that. It all just did not add up. The only rational explanation she could think of was that the wartime Adrian and Maria had children with the same names which would make her Adrian and Maria brother and sister but in that case Adrian would know where Maria was and wouldn't be looking for her.

The final cutting seemed irrelevant to Magda. It concerned a Mr. Thomas Barton who had a pig stolen from in his garden.

All she now knew for certain was that her cottage had once been called Lavender Cottage and its name was changed after a fire. She knew people were superstitious about things like that. Where there were fatal disasters, names were often changed or even buildings demolished. She thought of the home of Fred and Rose West in Cromwell Street, Gloucester. That building had been razed to the ground following its horrific revelations.

So, Maria and that Adrian had both been killed, one by a house fire and one shot down in the war. It made a kind of sense of the dreams. The imminent danger the sounds of shouting, the engine noise but not of why she was having them unless it was just because she was living in the place where these things happened.

Warily she looked round her comfortable lounge. There was no sense of menace at all. From the beginning she had felt at home here. But then she thought of Aymes and what Beth had said about a ghost. Was there one here? And was that why she was having the dreams? *No, ghosts made the atmosphere cold and menacing while the cottage felt warm and welcoming.* There had to be a rational explanation for all that was going on. She realised she had drunk the wine and her glass was empty. She went into the kitchen for a refill.

The dogs were still sleeping under their bush. The warm sun shone into the garden and the heady scent of the roses, lavender and various other shrubs and plants filled the air. The whole scene was one of contentment. There was nothing nasty here.

She set about preparing a meal, all the while thinking about Maria, the Maria who had lived here, the Maria who had probably cooked in this kitchen, bathed in this bathroom, sat in this garden. *Who actually was Maria?* Magda wished she knew.

The next day was Magda's appointment with Occupational Health so she got up early and got ready for her appointment. As she had thought it would it all went smoothly. She had blood taken and answered a questionnaire about her health. Finally, she saw the doctor who told her everything was in order and that she would get her confirmation letter with a start date within the next week.

I need this, Magda thought as she treated herself to a cup of tea and a sandwich in the *Sainsburys* café. *I'll be busy. I won't have time to fixate on Adrian. I can stop thinking about Maria.* By now, in her own mind she was beginning to see this obsession as part of her grieving process for Dennis.

Adrian she posited firmly to herself, *just wants to drop by now and again for a chat, and although it was tragic what happened to Maria Colleano, it's all just coincidence and nothing for me to dwell on.* With this established firmly in her mind, she drove back home.

Not wanting to sit and re-read the cuttings in her study, she got the dogs ready for another walk. She stopped off at the shop on the way back to buy a card to send to Beth.

Linda greeted her, looking distraught. 'Margaret's ill; she's had a stroke. She's gone to *Addenbrooke's.* Jim's gone there now.'

Magda found tears threatening as she remembered how sweet old Margaret Cooper had been to her. A pang of guilt struck too as she had not gone back to see her.

'Oh Linda, I'm so sorry. She's a lovely lady. She seemed strong too, so maybe she'll pull through.'

Linda sniffed back her own tears. 'She's very old though. It'll kill Jim if she dies. He's an only child you see. He adores his mum.'

'I'm really sorry. Please let me know if there's anything I can do. Do you need any help with the shop? I could try and give you a hand, but I don't know how much use I'd be.'

Linda smiled at this. 'No, really it's okay, my brother's coming down from Leicester. He used to run a small shop. He'll help out until Margaret's better or...'

She didn't finish but Magda knew she had been going to add *or dies.*

Magda felt sad all the way home. So much death seemed to surround her. Dennis, Maria and her Adrian and now maybe that sweet old lady. Once again Magda found herself wishing that Max was at home. She could have done with his cheerful company right now. But of course, his cottage remained empty for now. She hoped that he was having a good time and when she got in, she went to water his plants as promised.

That evening after dinner, she looked at the cuttings again, wondering why the piece about the man and the pig was with them. *Tom Barton? Did he live in one of the cottages here? Is there any connection? I can't see it.*

Firmly putting the cuttings away into the desk drawer in the study Magda wrote the postcard for Beth. She had tried to ring her friend the previous evening but there had been no reply. She was obviously still away so Magda had bought the card to send instead. *We never know what's in store* she thought as she put the stamp on and left it in the kitchen to take to the post when she walked the dogs the next day.

Chapter Fourteen

THE next morning after breakfast Magda got the dogs and went to the garage to post the card. As she walked on afterwards, she remembered the man, who had been cutting the hedges. She wondered then if the Thomas Barton in the cutting could have been him. She looked to see if she could spot his cottage, and yes, there it was over the other side of the river further along the bank. For a second she wondered how he got across. She hadn't noticed a bridge at all.

The dogs were enjoying themselves so she carried on further than she usually went and sure enough there was a small iron bridge. She crossed over and found herself quite near Thomas' cottage. He had asked her to call, so she thought that maybe she would. However, something stopped her. She wasn't sure it was right to just turn up, despite his invitation to do so. She longed to ask him about the pig though, so walked on in the direction of the cottage.

Luck was firmly on her side. As she got nearer, she saw him working in his garden which was beautiful, neat, tidy and comprised the most glorious display of well cared for plants. He was wearing his cap, which as before, he doffed on her arrival.

'Hello my dear, how lovely to see you and your two little beauties.' The dogs greeted him, as if he were an old friend.

'Were you looking for me?'

'Actually, I was. I was sent some newspaper cuttings the other day, about the cottage where I live. You were right, there was a fire there during the war. Seems like it was started deliberately too. Anyway, amongst the cuttings was one about a Thomas Barton who had a pig stolen.'

'Oh aye, that would be my father. We had this pig see, and we was fattening 'im up to eat. The war years was very lean and food very scarce, even round these parts. Anyway, one morning my dad got up and went to feed the pig and 'im 'ad gone – disappeared like. We never found 'im. My dad reckoned some bastard took 'im for the meat, but that were unusual round here like. Most folks was honest and we all knew one another. Didn't know it had made the papers though. Well I never.'

Tom contemplated this for a few moments. 'I remembers that poor old pig well. 'Enry we called 'im, after 'Enry the Eighth 'cos on the farm he 'ad lots of wives, see.'

Magda smiled at this as did Thomas.

'Would you like to come inside for a drink? I'll get a bowl of water for them dogs too.'

Not liking to refuse, Magda followed Thomas inside. His cottage, like his garden was beautiful. It was very small, but the furniture was antique and well cared for. It was a comfortable home too, Magda could tell. Thomas indicated a chair for her to sit down and he went out into the kitchen, closely followed by the two dogs. When he returned with a tray bearing cups and saucers, a tea pot, milk jug and plate of biscuits, Magda noticed the dogs were munching on something.

'I give 'em a couple of biscuits, hope you don't mind. They just be plain digestives like.' Thomas pointed to the ones on the plate.

'Oh, they would love that. You're very kind, thank you.'

'Not at all. I miss having a dog, but at my age wouldn't be fair on 'im see. I might not get out walking every day.' Thomas busied himself pouring the tea.

Magda had noticed a wedding photo on the sideboard. 'Is that you and your wife?' she asked.

'Oh aye, that be me and Eileen alright. She passed some seven years ago now.'

'I'm sorry. I know what it's like. My husband died in December.'

'My word, 'im was young to die.'

Magda found herself relating the circumstances of Dennis' death. When she had finished Thomas lent over and patted her hand.

'It's hard to lose someone sudden like.'

'Do you have children?'

'No, we was never blessed I'm afraid. But we meant the world to each other. Was cancer took 'er.'

Magda expressed her sorrow for him once again. They chatted together for a while. There was a grandmother clock in the corner which ticked rhythmically almost lulling Magda to sleep. Rousing herself she told him she should be going back.

'That's alright my dear. You come and see me anytime. I'm usually here.'

Magda thanked him for the tea and Thomas saw her out, bending down to pat both the dogs and then opening the gate to allow them through.

'You take care now my dear,' were his parting words as he walked back inside his cottage.

Magda felt almost as if she had entered another world inside his house. A quiet, peaceful, relaxed one. Something timeless about it. She crossed back over the bridge and set off for home where she spent most of the day reading in the garden. She was glad she had found out about the pig, but still wondered why the cutting had been in with the ones about the cottage. She shivered suddenly at the thought of there being a fire; her worst nightmare come true, for poor Maria.

Luckily, once again there were no disturbing dreams.

The next morning her contract arrived. Magda signed it and found an envelope in which to post it. She fed the dogs, had breakfast and set off for the garage, not sure if they were a post office or not. If not then she would need to go into Ramsey to post it as it was large and bulky.

When she arrived it became apparent that Linda had been crying. There was a tall, slightly stooped man standing next to her who smiled a greeting to Magda even though she was a stranger to him.

Linda lifted her reddened eyes and sniffing, told Magda that Margaret was not expected to live beyond the day. Magda was saddened and told Linda so. Linda then in turn introduced her brother 'Charles from Leicester,' and they shook hands.

Magda didn't like to ask about post office facilities as she could see how much Linda had on her mind. She decided to take the letter back and go into Ramsey instead. She paid her paper bill, told Linda again, just how sorry she was to hear about Margaret and bidding them both goodbye, left the shop for her normal walk with the dogs down to the river.

Later on she set off in the car to Ramsey and posted the contract, returning home with a spot of necessary shopping. Once again the day was hot and airless so she watered Max's plants and her own before settling in the garden with her book.

The next thing she was aware of was being woken by a hand on her shoulder and she found Adrian standing over her, looking concerned.

'I say, are you okay? You were shouting in your sleep.'

Mortified Magda struggled to a sitting position and hastily tried to smooth her clothes and hair. Her hair, always with a mind of its own, was straggling across her face, having escaped from its loose knot of the morning. She felt completely wrong-footed.

'Oh hello, yes, I'm alright thanks.' She had no intention then of telling him what she'd been dreaming about – horrors involving him – afraid she'd upset him.

Once again he refused the offer of refreshments and to Magda it seemed rude to go in and get one for herself, despite feeling in desperate need of a cup of tea.

He sat down next to her but remained silent and Magda, still reeling slightly from the dream and Adrian's sudden and unexpected presence did not know how to break the silence. Her mind went round and round like a hamster on a wheel, searching for something to say, to break the ice. Then she noticed Rollins.

He was standing under a nearby bush, making a low, but distinctly threatening growl in the back of his throat. If Adrian were aware of the little dog, he made no mention of it.

Magda had never heard Rollins growl before, let alone with his hackles raised. Then he leapt past and shot into the house. Again there was absolutely no sign of his brother and they were usually inseparable.

'I think I'll just go in and get a cup of tea and check on the dogs. Are you sure you wouldn't like one?'

Adrian smiled, shaking his head.

Magda walked inside but there was no sign of either of the dogs. She made a quick cup of tea and took it back outside, standing in the doorway to watch Adrian for a second. He sat absolutely still and there was such a calmness about him. He seemed totally at ease with himself, very different from the first time she had met him when he had been searching for Maria. *Maybe he's found her* she thought suddenly. This brought her an odd mixture of joy and sadness. If he had indeed found Maria, would he still visit? She very much wanted him to.

She sat down and began to sip her tea and after a while Adrian began to talk. He spoke of generalities, the weather; the garden and asked after her health. It seemed such a stilted and one-sided conversation it frustrated Magda. Surely by now they should have progressed beyond such small talk.

As the sky darkened and night fell, they fell into a more comfortable rhythm of conversation. Adrian seemed to have endless stories of his childhood, but it was as if his life had finished after that. He didn't talk about anything recent. However, Magda hung on his every word, finding pleasure in listening to the cadence of his voice, very much as she had when she listened to Dennis. There was something restful for her in the sound of his voice.

It became chillier, and Magda needed to move. 'It must be quite late,' she said. Then she cursed herself, not wanting him to leave.

'That's fine. The sun's gone and it's getting cool.' He rose and turned to leave.

Magda moved towards him and for a second their eyes met but she was unable to read what was there and hesitated just a moment too long.

'Thank you for a lovely evening.'

He did not even take her hand. With that parting remark, he turned, walked up the path, out of the gate and was gone.

He's such an exasperating man, Magda thought as she went inside.

Chapter Fifteen

THE following days were uneventful. The weather held and Magda and the dogs went on lots of long walks. Beth returned from her friend's and Magda and the dogs went to Highgate for the day to visit. As she neared her old flat Magda found herself crying for Dennis, the loss hitting her hard once again. She remained in the car to compose herself and do some damage limitation to her red-rimmed eyes.

Beth was delighted to see both her and the little dogs. They raced in and greeted her like the long-lost friend she had become. She in turn greeted them ecstatically before turning and hugging Magda.

'My goodness, you're brown as a berry,' she exclaimed. 'Must be all that country air.'

Magda agreed it was, and that yes, she did spend a lot of her time outside.

Beth settled the dogs with a filled bone each and poured a cup of strong coffee for Magda. Magda remembered the taste of Beth's coffee and this again reminded her of the days following Dennis' death, when Beth had insisted that Magda come down to her flat at least once a day. She had always had coffee percolating in the kitchen.

'How's your friend now?' asked Magda and Beth said she was slightly better but the hospital were saying she could not go home to live alone again so Beth was contemplating asking her to move in with her. Apparently the Axelrods were on the move again as he had been offered a job in Canada and Beth was pleased as said she had not really warmed to them as neighbours.

'I don't suppose you would like to come back?'

Magda shook her head vehemently at this. 'Oh no, I'm done with London. Anyway, I haven't told you, I've got a job. I start in September.'

Beth was delighted by this and was very stalwart in declaring that Magda would be brilliant. While Beth went to make them some lunch Magda reflected on how lucky she was to have such friends as Beth, Janette and Max. Without them her life would have become very bleak after Dennis.

This of course led her on to think of Adrian. Strangely she had not seen him since that last time and had had no further dreams either. Maybe that was the Universe telling her to forget all that had gone on since she moved into Hornbeams.

Beth came bustling back with their sandwiches and plates of chicken for the two dogs, who fell on them ravenously.

When they had all eaten, they went for a long walk in Highgate Woods. Beth seemed to manage very well as long as she used her elegant walnut walking stick with the silver fox head handle. Magda remarked on how lovely it was and Beth told her it had been her late husband's. Then they began to talk about their losses and how these had affected both their lives. Far from making them feel sad, this sharing seemed to cheer them up, giving them common cause in their efforts to move on with their lives.

Magda found herself then telling Beth all about Adrian.

'He sounds a fascinating man.' Beth commented when Magda finished. 'He must feel something for you or he wouldn't keep coming round. Men make friends very easily my dear. He wouldn't have need of another friend in you, I wouldn't think, so it has to mean something more.'

This felt like music to Magda's ears. She hoped her older friend with all her worldly experience was right in what she was saying. She went home later that day feeling boosted by such a lovely time with her friend.

She dreamt again that night. Exactly the same scenario; the running, the terror, the flames, was all there in terrifying *Technicolour*, like a late-night horror film.

When she woke, she'd tangled the duvet all round her body and was lying half out of the bed.

It took a while for the fear to subside. When it did, she got up and went downstairs. Looking out of the kitchen window she noticed a light on in Max's house and realised that it was the day he was due to return. His presence there made her feel somewhat calmer. She had been in earlier to put some bread, butter, milk and cheese in his fridge, to put a bouquet of freshly-cut flowers from her garden on his kitchen table and to leave a bottle of wine on the table. All things to say *Welcome home*.

For a second or two she contemplated going over and knocking on his door, but reasoned that as he could have only just got in, the last thing he would need would be her in this state of mind.

Wearily, with tea in hand, she mounted the stairs to bed. A glance at the bedside clock read 2.17 so she was glad she had not succumbed to the temptation to bother Max. Sleep, however, continued to elude her.

She lay there taking stock. She had a job now, she had her home, her dogs; lovely friends like Beth so why couldn't she just drift into peaceful sleep each night? She thought about Beth and the ghost. Surely not? A ghost wouldn't invade dreams. It would manifest as something cold in the house, something nasty. This house was friendly, warm, inviting. She remembered the day the dogs had found it. How it seemed to call to her, that it was meant to be her home. How anxious she had felt dialling the estate agent, worrying that they would tell her it had been sold. No, this was her home it was meant to be.

She snuggled down then, with the reassuring thought of Max being back next door and Janette along at the end. Nothing nasty could get her while she had lovely people like that looking out for her. *You're being silly, over emotional*, she told herself as sleep gradually beckoned.

The next morning, as she was picking some flowers to put on the kitchen window sill a head popped over the fence. 'Buongiorno or Bonjour from Corsica.' All Magda could see was a straw hat, a hand holding a bottle of wine wrapped in raffia and a large baguette waving at her.

'Welcome home Max.'

'How the devil did you know it was me?'

'Well the *from Corsica* bit for a start, coupled with the fact that you live next door.'

Max chuckled as he made an unusual entrance for him, actually using the gate. 'I come bearing gifts. Look wine, bread, cheese. What more could a lady ask for?'

Before she had time to think about it, Magda found herself hugging him. Even before taking the gifts out of his hands.

'Come on, sit down on one of the garden chairs. How was it? How many broken hearts have you left in your wake?'

'Ah my dear you grace me with too many charms. The days of leaving broken hearts behind are long gone.'

'Oh, for goodness sake, you're a youngster yet. Come on, I bet some fine Corsican ladies are bemoaning your leaving as we speak.'

Once again Max chuckled. 'Well I don't think much of the service round here. Come on girl, get that wine open.'

Magda looked at her watch. It was gone one she was surprised to note. The morning seemed to have fled past unnoticed. *Probably due to my broken night*, she thought as she took the offerings from Max and went inside to make them some lunch.

'Thank you for the things you left in my fridge. I suppose it was you, or was it Janette?'

'No, that was me. Couldn't have you coming home to bare cupboards. Didn't know of course that you'd be bringing your own supplies.'

'What do you think of the cheese? It's local to where I was staying.'

Magda took a bite of the sliced baguette on which she had spread the slightly runny cheese.

'Mmmm it's lovely, thank you. Very ripe.'

'How polite we are today. Yes, it suffered a little from being in my backpack.'

Magda smiled. It felt so good to have Max home. Then suddenly she was pierced with an uncomfortable thought. Supposing Adrian decided to call unexpectedly and found her here having lunch with Max. She went hot and cold just thinking about it. So engrossed was she that she missed what Max had been saying.

'Earth to Magda.' Max nudged her shoulder.

'Oh, sorry Max, been having some disturbed nights recently. Sorry.'

Max looked concerned. 'Why what's been going on? No nocturnal visitors I hope?' He looked at her quizzically.

Suddenly Magda felt shy. She had wanted Max home so she could confide in him, but now faced with him, she felt tongue-tied and unable to explain. Instead she busied herself eating. Max remained silent but the atmosphere felt strained because she knew he was waiting for her to explain.

Once they had finished their lunch, Max looked across at her with a questioning smile. 'So come on then, tell Uncle Max what's been going on?'

'Oh Max, it's nothing really, just I am still having those dreams; you know, the ones I told you about. With the airbase and the woman. They come regularly and they frighten me to be honest. Then there's Adrian. He's such a strange man.'

'I take it he's been round here then?'

Magda nodded.

'He has and he seems so sad and so lost. He's been telling me about his past and his family. He grew up in Wiltshire, near Box. He seems to get close but then he pulls away. I don't understand him at all.'

'Well the thing you need to ask yourself, my dear, is do you want him close? What kind of a relationship do you want with our mysterious airman?'

Magda took time to consider her answer.

'I don't know. It's too soon, I think. Sometimes I confused the feelings I have for Adrian and those I have for Dennis. Then the dreams come and I get the feeling he's connected to them somehow. How I don't know. I found out some things online and Mrs Grigson's son sent over some newspaper clippings he found here. They mention an Adrian Taylor-Beaumont but the dates don't add up. He'd be over eighty if he was still alive. Then there's all that about Maria, although to be honest Adrian hasn't mentioned her lately. Would you like to see what I've found out?'

Max nodded and Magda went inside to get them. She rummaged through the papers in her study finding only the ones relating to her new job. *Oh, I must mention my job to Max*, she thought as she opened drawers. However, the newspaper cuttings were nowhere to be seen. *They have to be here*, she thought, in a panic as she rifled through the drawers again and again but there was no sign of them. She walked over to the window sill to see if she had left them there but they weren't there so she abandoned the study and went up to her bedroom. Nothing!

Sighing, Magda went back down and out into the garden.

'Oh, Max I can't find them. I know I left them in the study, but they seem to have disappeared.'

'Oh, Magda calm down. They'll turn up and you can show me then.'

Magda realised then how distraught she had sounded.

Max poured them both another glass of wine. 'I tell you what. I'm a professor of history. You know that of course, don't you? Well I have access to lots of resources. Would it help you if I tried to find this Maria for you?'

'I forgot to say, there was a fire here; here in this cottage. They think it was arson too. I've felt so scared since I found that out. I hate fire. It's a bit of a phobia to be honest. Then there's Aymes, and my friend Beth, you know, my old neighbour, she asked if there could be a ghost.' Magda knew she was babbling but somehow it all seemed to be gushing out. As she voiced it, she became aware just how scared she had been while Max was away. Putting her head into her hands she began to sob.

Max got up, put his arms round her and held her. This only made her cry harder. She realized just how long it had been since someone had held and comforted her. Nobody since she lost Dennis. Beth had been the nearest but there had been no physical comfort, just emotional support.

Max continued to hold her while she sobbed.

'Oh dear, you've only just come back and you've made our Magda cry.'

Magda raised her head to find Janette standing there. Max smiled but

Magda noticed he shook his head at Janette as if to say, *Not now, no jokes.* Janette, always quick on the uptake, caught on straight away and sitting down on the chair next to Magda, she took Magda's hand in her own.

'Probably good to let it all out love. I wondered when the storm might hit. You've been through two of the things professionals consider the most stressful life events; bereavement and moving house. You've been so strong and so together, but now and again it's bound to hit. You know both Max and I are here for you and it's a safe space to grieve.'

Magda could do nothing but nod.

Max whipped a pristine white handkerchief from his trouser pocket, which he handed to her with a flourish. 'There you go my dear, use this to mop yourself up.'

Gratefully Magda took it and wiped her eyes.

'Look, now you may think I'm being harsh and it may not be what you want to hear, but I think you have become a bit fixated on this whole thing. We know nothing about Adrian and the fact that he keeps just turning up leads me to believe he could be a bit of a rum sort. The whole Maria thing too, that's made you feel sad. I know it has. Magda, my sweet. I'm only saying this because I care. I know we haven't known each other very long, but I feel as if we have known each other forever and if I'm not mistaken I think Janette feels the same.' Janette nodded her agreement. 'We've become a little, close-knit family if you ask me. These cottages do have a special feel to them too. I think it's because there are only four and we are pushed together. So why don't you, if you want to, that is, invite this Adrian fellow to have dinner with me and Janette? We can give him the once over.'

Once again Janette nodded.

Magda gave a shuddering sigh as finally the tears abated. 'I don't know. Oh, maybe. I don't know.'

Max chuckled. 'Just think about it, darling girl, and Janette and I will be ready to come to the crease. You just have to say the word.'

Magda returned his hug. 'Thank you. Thank you, my dear friend, for being so kind to me. I feel the same, like we're all a family. Goodness, I don't know what I would have done if you two hadn't been living here. Gone mad probably.' She gave Janette a wry smile.

'Have you told Max your good news?'

'No, not yet. I was about to when I got a bit overwhelmed. But Max, I've been offered a job. Part time, working at the same place as Janette.'

'Well that's just brilliant. Well done you. So, tonight we must definitely celebrate. Come on it'll be fun. My place...say eight, the pair of you and I'll cook you a meal.'

Magda caught the look of concern on Janette's face when he used the word *cook*. Obviously, she had sampled Max's cooking before and found it somewhat wanting by the look of it.

'No, Max, you've just come back from holiday. You won't have much in. Come to mine instead and all you two need to bring is the wine. And yourselves of course.' Janette downed the last of her wine and stood up. 'I'll go home and see what I can rustle up for us. You okay now Magda?'

Magda nodded. 'Yes, fine now and thanks again for being here for me.'

'Well as the saying goes that's what friends are for,' and Janette planted a kiss on top of Magda's head before she left.

The evening was great fun and when Magda and Max staggered home it was almost two in the morning.

'Night my darling, sleep well.' Max called out as he vaulted the garden fence.

'Night Max, you too.' Magda found her door key and let herself in. Rollins raced to greet her and she opened the back door for him to go into the garden. She called Aymes but he did not appear.

'Where's your brother eh?' Magda fondled Rollins' ears as she waited for Aymes to materialise.

Finally, she heard him creeping down the stairs. He crawled across the kitchen almost on his stomach, like a soldier in combat, checking out the enemy. 'What is it boy?' Magda scooped him up into her arms where he stayed panting. 'What do you see or feel here?' She wished Aymes could tell her. She walked out into the garden and gently placed him down next to his favourite bush. Aymes sniffed around then raised his leg.

'Good boy, now who's for a treat?' Magda found the tin with their biscuits and handed them a *Bonio* each. She was gratified when Aymes took his and raced off to eat it. There was seldom a thing wrong with his appetite.

Although it was late Magda did not feel tired. They had enjoyed themselves and laughed so much as Max related details of his holiday and his supposed conquests! She made herself a cup of tea and then went into the lounge. The answerphone was flashing indicating a message. When she played it, it was Beth saying how much she had enjoyed their visit and before she finished asking how the ghost was.

Magda smiled. She was feeling better about all of it since this afternoon and what she now thought of as her *mini meltdown*. She was determined not to become obsessed with either Maria or Adrian. This was her home now, not Maria's, whoever she was, and Magda was going to enjoy living in it. Buoyed up by the support of her friends and now with the thought of work, she turned off the lights and went up to bed.

Of course, the dream came back.

Once again she ran along the road with the ghostly figure running beside her. Again, she saw her long, thick black hair streaming out behind her and, like Magda, seemed to have nothing on her feet and Magda could feel the harshness of the stones biting into hers. 'Aspetta, aspetta' the woman was shouting once again. 'Sono Italiana, non sono Tedesco.'

Magda thought the first bit meant, *I'm Italian* but wasn't sure. There was so much distress in that voice. Just then there was an explosion and in front of them a fireball coming towards them. Magda could feel the heat and see the orange and red flames as they flickered within the huge orb.

The woman was screaming and screaming and then it all went black.

Magda woke sweating and screaming. She lay there panting. It was some time before she felt able to pull herself together. The duvet was in a heap, on the floor, Rollins was sandwiched between the two pillows next to Magda's and there was no sign of Aymes.

Magda got out of bed and peered underneath. There he was, curled into a ball. He didn't want to come out though, so she left him there, satisfied that he was okay.

She took a deep breath and looked at the clock. It was twenty past four, far too early to get up. Her throat felt parched but she put that down to the amount of wine they had drunk earlier. She wished she had remembered to drink some water before going to bed but the thought of going down to the kitchen seemed impossible. She felt as if she didn't dare; scared by what she might see. *This is ridiculous* she told herself sternly but instead of going downstairs she went into the little en-suite where she found her tooth mug, filled it with water and drank it all down. Then she refilled it and did the same. Her throat continued to feel as if it had been burned and she was surprised that her feet were unhurt. The stones she had trodden had seemed just so real as they bit into her tender soles. *Am I going mad?* She wondered as reluctantly she went back to bed.

Rollins came out and snuggled down next to her. Gently she stroked his soft fur and gradually her heartrate returned to normal and she slipped back into sleep.

Chapter Sixteen

STRANGELY over the next few weeks there was no sign of Adrian and even more strangely, no more dreams. The house felt peaceful like it had when first Magda moved into it. With the absence of both she began to relax and become more like her old self. She had a date too for starting her job, the fifteenth of September just two weeks away. Phil had sent her another lovely welcoming letter with details of her hours. She would be working Wednesday, Thursday and Friday each week from nine thirty until four thirty. Just right she thought.

Janette was over the moon and suggested they share transport on the days Magda was due to work. 'We could have a kind of rota. I'll drive one week, Magda and you the next, what do you think?'

'Sounds good to me.'

They sealed the deal with a cup of tea.

The weather continued to remain dry and when Magda went to the paper shop, she found Linda sorrowful and red eyed. 'Margaret passed away last weekend. It was very peaceful.'

Magda found her own eyes filling with tears.

'She left this for you.' Linda was riffling around under the counter from which she pulled an envelope. 'Think it's something that happened at your place, you know, like she was telling you. Anyway, she found this and thought you might like it.'

Magda took the envelope and telling Linda how sorry she was for her loss, left the shop. When she got home, she opened the envelope and inside were some of the same newspaper cuttings Mrs Grigson's son had sent. Margaret too must have kept them for some reason. There was a photo of what seemed to be her cottage, although it looked very different. It was just a burnt-out shell. *Oh god!* Magda was shocked. How awful that this lovely home had undergone something like that. When she had heard about the fire, she had not imagined that amount of damage. It would have had to have been almost completely re-built. *How sad.* It repeated what the earlier clippings had said, that the sole inhabitant, a Miss Maria Colleano, aged twenty-three, had died there.

Magda found her hands were shaking as she read through the article. Miss Colleano it had been thought was of German origin but turned out to have been Italian in fact.

Sono Italiana. The words from Magda's dream hit her like a thud to the chest. That had to have been the Maria who died in my cottage, she thought, as shakily she returned the cuttings to the envelope. She found the number for the little store and rang it. Linda answered.

'Oh, hello it's Magda. I was wondering; I know I only met her once, but could I attend Margaret's funeral? I would really like to.'

'Oh, bless you Magda, how kind. Sorry love but its family only, Margaret specified that in her will. She'll be buried in Ramsay churchyard next to Fred, her husband. Perhaps you could lay some flowers on her grave. She loved flowers and loved the ones you took her. She was full of them when me and Jim visited after you were there.'

'Thank you, Linda, I will. Next time I go into Ramsay I'll take some from the garden. That's what I took before.'

With that Magda rang off. She had indeed liked the elderly woman who had been open with her and willing to share some of her past. Thinking of the grave made her think of Dennis. She vowed to herself to go and lay some flowers on his grave soon. She had shied away from visiting it but now felt it was time and she could cope.

Magda put the cuttings back into the envelope and when she went to put them away in the study was amazed to see the ones Mrs Grigson's son had sent, all lying just where she had thought she put them. *How odd*, she thought as she put all of them together. *I know I looked there, more than once and I swear they weren't there.*

As much as she tried that evening, she could not get those words out of her head *Sono Italiana*. Eventually she fired up her laptop and Googled them. They meant just what she had thought they meant. *So, why had men been chasing her? What had happened? And were they the people who had set the fire?* The thoughts made her shiver. Not for the first time she wished Dennis was there with her, keeping her safe.

To take her mind of everything she began to look through the things Phil had sent. The job was pretty much what she had done in London. *Only two more weeks, then I can start. I can focus on my clients, stop thinking about Maria and about Adrian. Maybe the dreams will stop too.* That cheered her as she went about preparing an evening meal.

The evenings were certainly drawing in. *I wonder what winter will be like here.* Magda thought as she took her lasagne and salad outside to sit and eat. *It will be cosy, I think. There's the brand-new boiler and the gas fire in the lounge. The dogs and I can snuggle down and keep warm. I hope the electricity doesn't cut out if there's snow.* Then she remembered the generator. *Yes, we are going to be snug and warm.* The seasons certainly were more noticeable here in the countryside she was sure. In London it was usually grey, rainy and slushy in winter although the colours of autumn in Highgate woods were magnificent. Magda pictured herself and the dogs snuggled on the settee with the gas fire glowing as if it were a real wood burner and the curtains drawn keeping out the cold and the night. It was an appealing vision of the future. Then despite vowing not to, her thoughts turned to Adrian. *Would he continue to visit when the summer was over or would he like the swallows, move on and leave? Only time will tell I suppose,* she thought as she went inside in search of ice cream.

The days until Magda was due to begin her job meandered on. Just as she had promised, she found Margaret's grave, just a newly dug mound of earth but she laid some flowers there anyway. She thought about Margaret lying next to her husband. *I wonder if I will lie beside Dennis,* she thought, *but no, I want to be cremated.* Not for her a burial with worms getting in and eating away at her. That made her sad, to think then of Dennis. She should have stood up to his mother and insisted on cremation. She had felt so weak though at the time.

Max went on another week's holiday, this time to Germany, and again Magda was asked if she minded looking after his garden and plants.

'Of course, I don't mind,' she agreed.

'Last ditch of freedom and then it's back to the coal face,' he laughed as he handed over the key. He said hadn't forgotten his promise though and had asked a mate at the Imperial War Museum to find out all he could about the airfield.

He arrived back with German sausages, which he insisted on cooking for her and Janette and as usual they had an uproarious evening together.

Then it was time for Magda to start her new job. The first morning Janette drove them in. She took Magda inside to the reception area and showed her where she had to tick herself in on the large white board hung up there.

'It's not that important as you'll be here all the time. However, we're all out and about and if there are phone calls, the ladies at the desk can tell people whether anyone is available or not.'

She introduced Magda to the two ladies at the desk and two others doing the typing. All seemed friendly and Cilla one of the receptionists rang up to the office to say that Magda had arrived.

Jenny came bustling down in person. 'Hi there Magda. Welcome. Come on up and I'll show you to your desk. We're upstairs in the attic I'm afraid.'

Magda said a hasty goodbye to Janette and followed Jenny up a flight of stairs.

At the top there were three doors and Jenny pushed open the second one. 'Here you go. That'll be your desk. Let me introduce you to everyone.' Magda saw that there were three desks on each side of the room. At the one next to hers there was a young man, probably in his early thirties. 'This is Ross,' Jenny beamed at her and Ross smiled and held out his hand.

'Hi Magda. Welcome to the funny farm.' She could tell immediately that they were going to get along.

'And this is Julie, our art therapist, and sitting there is Amy; she does CBT.'

Julie came over to shake her hand and Amy, who was busy on the phone, waved.

Magda noticed there was a large printed note attached to her desk, saying *Welcome Magda* and for one awful moment she thought she was going to cry. Hastily pushing back the tears, she sat down.

Ross gave her another beaming smile and showed her how to turn on her laptop. Everyone apart from Jenny had a laptop rather than a desktop computer. He was busy showing her the software and she didn't have the heart to tell him that it was the same as she had used in London. Instead she nodded along at all he told her.

'Fancy a cup of tea or coffee?' Jenny asked. 'I'll take you down to the team room. That's where we make drinks. I can introduce you then to anyone who's in. Have you brought a mug? We all tend to keep ours up here.'

Magda, forewarned of this by Janette delved into her large tote and produced her mug. 'I have.' She waved it at Jenny.

'Oh, look it's got a lovely dog on there. Do you have any pets Magda? I've got two cats and the kids have a rabbit each.' She didn't wait for Magda's answer.

They walked past reception and down a corridor. Each side there appeared to be what she thought were the treatment rooms and Magda wondered which would be hers. There was a door at the end which Jenny opened, standing aside to let Magda go through before her. There was a kind of corridor of a kitchen with a table and chairs in a small alcove and a sink on the other side. Further down, the room opened out into a large office space with desks at intervals all round, several of them occupied by people who looked up as one to see the new arrival.

Magda felt shy all of a sudden but Jenny introduced her as brightly as she had upstairs and once again everyone responded in a friendly fashion. Turning round in the open plan area she found Janette had her own corner. She was sitting at her desk grinning madly at Magda and giving her a thumbs up.

With all the introductions over, Jenny took her to the kitchenette to make tea which they took back upstairs.

Phil, who apparently occupied the small office next door, came in to shake her hand and to welcome her at that point. 'I'll organize some clients for you. Take it easy today, just get to know everyone and get familiar with things. We have the full team meeting this afternoon; that's with all of us. I plan to ease you in gently this week, so don't feel alarmed at all.'

Once again Magda was struck by how much she liked him. In fact, the whole place had a warm and friendly atmosphere. She gave up silent thanks to Dennis, who she felt sure had to have guided her movements since he left her so abruptly.

The rest of the day went just as smoothly and soon Magda began to feel at home in her new job.

From the beginning Magda was given interesting, if challenging clients and far from being unable to cope, she found she got back into the swing of things easily and had soon built up a good rapport with them. One she particularly took to; a lady of around her own age, Sarah, who had recently escaped from a very abusive marriage. She had a daughter of nineteen, who did not live with her. Sarah was timid and eager to please, but gradually under Magda's guidance began to come out of her shell.

Summer blended into autumn and as Magda had predicted she and the dogs felt warm and cosy in the little cottage. Magda, Janette and Max had got into the habit of meeting once a week in each other's homes for dinner and a good chat and Magda began to think less and less about Adrian. There had been no sign of him since before she started her job. Like the swallows, he too had disappeared.

The Griffiths came down one weekend to pack things up. Gemma of course wanted to walk the dogs and even Justin accompanied them on the day they were going home.

'Jus has a crush on you.' Gemma whispered as they returned home.

Magda found herself blushing. She had never seen herself as the *Mrs Robinson* type!

Chapter Seventeen

IT was quite a surprise when at one of their gatherings Max brought out some photocopies of things his friend had discovered about the cottages and the airfield.

With trembling hands Magda took them from him. She had felt so settled and peaceful lately, she wasn't sure she really wanted to know all that had gone on.

Curiosity, however, got the better of her and when the other two had gone she took the papers and a cup of tea up to bed, nestling down into the pillows, with Rollins by her side.

The first thing she learned was that there had definitely been a small airfield just where the Tesco Express shop was now. It had been decommissioned after the war. Missions were flown to Germany from it and there had been many casualties among the pilots. Nothing too unusual about that although Magda felt a pang for those brave men who had risked their lives for their country.

The next document had more personal relevance. It detailed the fire at the cottage, which it said, had been set by five men, who believed the occupant to be a German spy having an affair with one of the pilots. Where the rumour started, nobody seemed to know but it culminated in her cottage being set on fire in December 1944. Later it had been revealed that the woman was not German, but Italian. She had come to the country as a refugee from Minori, a village in the South of Italy.

Magda turned over one of the pages and gasped. There, in rather grainy black and white, was the woman from her dreams. The same small heart-shaped face, the long cloud of curly black hair. It was her! Underneath was printed the name Maria Colleano.

Magda felt as if the room was spinning.

Maria Colleano was the lady Adrian sought, however impossible that was. In 1944, this Maria looked to be in her early twenties. She would be in her eighties or nineties now. *She must have had a daughter*, Magda thought. *Maria had to have had a daughter, also named Maria and she's the one Adrian's looking for.* There was no other explanation.

Further delving into the papers showed pictures of the cottage after it had been burned, just as in the old newspapers. The article went on to say that Mr Thomas Barton had called the fire brigade who were already out on a call but came as soon as they could. Sadly, it had been too late to save the occupant. On the next page was a photograph of the old airfield with the wind sock billowing out. There were hangars and several men working on planes. The photograph's annotation stated that it had been taken by one of the pilots, a Mr. Wilfred Barrington.

Magda felt totally drained as she looked at the final paper. It showed the little group of cottages as they had been before the fire. Magda felt as if she had run a marathon and once again her heart was pounding. Rollins licked her hand – Aymes, as always, was hiding under the bed.

Whatever's going on? Magda found herself thinking. The more she learned the odder it all became. *No,* she told herself firmly, *it is not odd. Maria must have had a daughter and she was the lady that Adrian knew. Nothing sinister, nothing nasty, nothing strange at all. But then why am I having all those dreams?*

Admittedly she'd not had one of the really frightening dreams for some weeks now, but nevertheless the woman she had seen in them was definitely Maria Colleano.

Wearily, she got out of bed and went to clean her teeth. She found herself looking into the mirror, almost expecting to see Maria standing behind her. *Stop it,* she told herself sternly. *You are imagining things and you have to stop.* She carried her toothbrush back into the bedroom and stood it on its charger. As she looked around the room she felt as if there were shadows everywhere. Shadows haunting her and telling her of the awful events of the past. *It's ridiculous,* she thought. *Mrs Grigson's son had this whole place done out. There can't be anything of the past left here. Okay, maybe the collective memory, but that's it. No ghosts, no hauntings, nothing like that at all.* She burrowed down into her bed and tried to sleep but sleep was, of course, elusive. She was far too wound up. *Thank goodness tomorrow's Saturday and I don't have to get up,* she thought as she crawled out of bed to go down and make a drink.

In the kitchen she looked out to see if Max was awake, feeling a desperate need for company, but his cottage was in darkness.

As she had known would be the case, in the morning Magda felt drained and listless. If it had not been for the dogs, scratching at her, wanting to be let out, she might have just huddled down and slept all day. Instead, she, dragged on her dressing gown and followed them downstairs and to the back door. They rushed off and Magda turned to fill the kettle.

As she glanced out of the window, she glimpsed someone out there. Wondering if it could be Adrian, she shrank back, not wanting him to see her looking as she did, so haggard and weary. When warily she peeked out, there was nobody there.

Two mugs of coffee did little to energise her, so Magda spent most of the morning reading. She didn't even bother to go and have a shower until after eleven o'clock.

When she took Rollins and Aymes for their walk, it seemed to her that autumn was here with a vengeance. Magda wondered how things could change so fast. Gone were those hot, long, lazy summer days and in their place was a landscape which seemed shrouded in mist and murk. Cobwebs shimmered on the bushes and leaves squelched under her feet. The dogs, however, raced around as usual.

Magda caught sight of Tom over on the other side of the river, standing outside his cottage. He was standing there staring into space and she wondered what he might be thinking. She gave him a wave but he was just too far away to notice her and Magda felt her melancholy mood matched the autumnal conditions as she and the dogs trudged onwards.

What did cheer Magda was spotting Max in his garden and the warmth of his greeting.

'Hi there. How were those press cuttings? Any good? Fancy a spot of lunch?'

Magda did not need asking twice. She took the dogs inside and settled them with a chew apiece, before leaving them to it.

'Come on in. Have a seat. Getting a bit chilly out there isn't it?'

Magda nodded. 'I was thinking just that. I can't believe all those lovely long summer days have gone.'

'Hey there, you don't sound like you. Is everything okay?'

Once again Magda was overwhelmed by Max's astuteness at picking up on her mood.

'Just a disturbed night, nothing major.'

'Anything to do with those cuttings? If so, I am sorry. I hesitated before giving them to you, to be honest. I thought the bit about the cottage might upset you.'

'It was awful to see it. However, it looks exactly the same as the other three now, so whomever renovated it first, did so sympathetically and I'm eternally grateful to Mrs. Grigson's son for how cosy he made it.'

Max placed a sandwich in front of her and busied himself pouring tea. He placed two mugs down on the table and sat down.

'Do you sometimes feel you were drawn here Max? That this was where you were meant to live?'

Magda had no idea why she had voiced her thoughts, but she had, and Max took time to answer.

'To be honest no. My wife chose this cottage but when our marriage went south I was determined to stay on living here. That was rather unlike me. I have always been a bit of a wanderer but this place took hold of me. I'd met Janette too of course and we got on so well. Then poor old Mrs G was here as well and I felt I couldn't abandon her, but nothing supernatural or strange made me want to stay if that's what you're thinking.'

It had been but suddenly Magda felt too shy to confess her thoughts.

'Max may I ask you something? And it's really okay if you don't want to. Would you come with me to Dennis' grave? I want to lay flowers there and to be honest I've never been back to see it. I wanted him to be cremated you see, but his family are staunchly Catholic and I gave in and agreed to a burial. I've regretted it ever since to be honest. I think that's been the main reason I haven't been. I had a headstone placed there but I've only seen that it in the catalogue when I chose it.' Magda was very close to tears.

Max leant over and patted her hand.

'Of course, I'll come with you my dear girl. It would be an honour. When would you like to go?'

Magda let out a breath she had not even been aware she was holding. Suddenly it seemed very important she go to the grave. It would give her closure, that oft misused term, she thought, welcoming the warmth of Max's hand over hers. 'Would tomorrow be too soon?'

'Not at all. In fact, I was just about to suggest it.'

'I could introduce you to Beth too. She's my old neighbour. She got me through after, you know...when Dennis had gone.'

Max was too much of a gentleman to ask why Magda had not chosen Beth to accompany her. So, with the arrangements in place the two of them sat and ate their sandwiches and Max chatted about his work and how hopeless and hapless some of his current students were. 'Never mind. I'll soon whip them into shape.' This lightened the rather sombre mood and Magda found herself laughing along.

After they had eaten, Magda excused herself and went home. En-route she stopped at Janette's so Magda could ask if she would mind looking in on the dogs the next day. 'I'm...I'm going up to London tomorrow. I need to see Dennis's grave and Max has kindly agreed to come with me.' Her voice sounded strangled as she told her friend.

'Oh Magda, of course I'll look in on the dogs. Are you sure you want to go?' Magda had already told her friend how she had given in over the burial and how sad she had subsequently felt too.

'Yes, it's time. I need to kind of draw a line under my old life, if you see what I mean?

Janette did. She had felt the same way after her divorce.

With that settled Magda wandered home.

After her disturbed night Magda felt tired. *I think an early night is in order,* she thought. She took a ready meal from the freezer, stabbed the cellophane and placed it in the oven and found some oven chips to go with it.

She fed the dogs and then let them out. A low mist had formed and the clouds were scudding busily by now and again obscuring the crescent moon that hung there like a child's toy up in the sky. 'I love you Dennis.' Magda whispered up at the sky, before turning around and shutting the back door.

Magda was in bed by nine, cuddled up with the dogs, a cup of tea, and the television for a dose of *Casualty* which she thought would bring a bit of normality to the day. She was just getting to an exciting part when there was a loud knock at the door.

Magda ignored it at first, but it was persistent and so, cursing, she got out of bed, grabbed her winter dressing gown, an old, worn, mauve fleecy thing she had had for years, shrugged it on and stomped down the stairs.

She flung open the door, about to yell at whoever had disturbed her tranquillity, only to find Adrian standing with his fist poised to knock again.

'Oh' was the only word she could find. Immediately she felt conscious of the fact that underneath her dressing gown she had on only the shorts and strappy top that she slept in. Her hair, was all over the place too from lying on the pillows. Not the kind of impression she really wanted to make!

'I'm sorry, did I disturb you?'

It was so obvious that he had but all Magda could do was give a little shake of the head.

'Come in.'

He hesitated. 'No, I couldn't possibly. You were obviously ready to go to bed.'

Magda realised just how much she had missed those upper class clipped tones, and his rather old-fashioned gentlemanly ways.

'It's okay, I can go and throw on some clothes. That's not a problem.'

Somehow it seemed desperately important that he should come inside.

Adrian however was standing there with a look almost of horror on his face. 'Goodness me no. I would never disturb a lady when she is in deshabille.'

Magda had to smile. It was as if he came from another world. 'Honestly you're really welcome. Do come in. It's so cold now outside.'

Adrian hesitated but then turned away. 'Sorry to have disturbed you.' He gave his usual little wave, and slipped out of the garden gate.

Magda slammed the door in frustration. 'God he's weird' she found herself shouting at the closed door.

As if Adrian had brought them, the dreams began again that night. The whole thing back bringing Magda back to heart-pounding awareness of reality and there was a raw feeling in the back of her throat as if she had been too near to something burning.

As always, it took Magda a few minutes to orientate herself. Gradually her bedroom came into view. The apricot walls, the cream curtains, her familiar furniture around and Rollins fast asleep on the bed beside her.

It was six-thirty. She had arranged to be ready for Max at nine so there was no point in trying to go back to sleep and anyway she felt an extreme reluctance to try. Instead she got up and went downstairs.

The kitchen was lovely and warm thanks to the new boiler, and when she let out the dogs, she gasped in awe at the sight of the frost that brushed all the shrubs and tree branches. Autumn it would seem, had given way to winter overnight. Well of course, it was well into November.

Magda hustled the dogs inside and gently shut the door. Bonfire night had passed unnoticed not like in London where there were fireworks for weeks both before and after the event. Trick or Treat too had taken off there and Magda and Dennis had always stocked a large tin of sweets for the revellers when they knocked. No need for that in the wilds of Cambridgeshire. Magda smiled as she thought of all the ghosts, vampires and witches she had served at their front door over the years. Nothing like that disturbed them here in their little enclave. The peace and quiet had allowed winter to sneak in unheralded.

Chapter Eighteen

ON the dot of nine Max knocked on her door.

'Ready, my dear? Ready to brave the big smoke?'

Magda smiled knowing everything was going to be all right; the day was going to go well. She nodded as she grabbed her coat and handbag from the rack by the door.

'Shall I be chauffeur?' Max asked cheerfully and Magda was only too pleased to let him drive. They chatted throughout the journey with *Radio Two* playing softly in the background.

Reaching London, Magda directed Max to the cemetery. She felt a chill go through her as they walked along the path surrounded by gravestones. *I'm not even sure where it is*, she thought in a moment of sheer panic but, as if by magic, her footsteps led her straight to where Dennis lay buried.

'It's here Max, just here.' Magda called him over.

Gently she began to place the flowers she had brought into a little stone cup with holes in the top. 'Hello my darling, she whispered as she arranged them. 'I miss you so much. But I have made two lovely friends. You would love them too. They've been so kind to me.' She was aware of Max standing just behind her, but didn't care. She wanted Dennis to know she was coping, getting on with life. Unaware that tears were pouring down her face, she continued to tell him about her new life, the dogs, her home, her job.

When she was done, she stood and gently kissed on her hand which she then transferred onto the marble headstone. The headstone was tasteful, black marble with silver lettering Max read the words aloud; 'Dennis Patrick McClean, beloved husband of Magda, son to Margaret and Patrick and brother to Roisin. May you Rest in Peace.' He found it touching and had a job not to allow a tear to fall. Magda, despite not getting along with her in-laws had done something so kind for them in recognising them on the stone.

Sensing she was done, he gently he whispered to her. 'Come along old thing, let's go and find that old neighbour of yours. I don't know about you, but I'm dying for a cuppa.'

Magda gave him a watery smile as they wandered back down the rows of graves, towards the car. Much to Magda's relief Max was silent throughout the short journey, allowing her to deal with her own thoughts. Flitting through her mind came memories; memories of meeting Dennis, their time spent together getting to know each other before he proposed, then the years they had spent together. Of course, like every married couple, there had been disagreements but theirs had always been short lived and soon forgotten. Suddenly, as clear as day, an image of Adrian flashed into her mind. Magda felt annoyed. After the way he had been last night she did not want him intruding into her thoughts. When she was reminiscing over her life with Dennis, he had no right to butt in.

When they arrived at her old road, there were no parking spaces. It being a Sunday most of the residents were home. Max drove round until he spotted a space, manoeuvring smartly into it and Magda fumbled in the back for the bunch of flowers she had brought for Beth.

As they walked down the street to Magda's old home, Max raised his eyebrows as if to say *All okay?* And Magda nodded.

Beth was, of course, overjoyed to see Magda and to meet Max. 'Oh how lovely. Do come in and how lovely to meet you Max. I've heard so much about you from Magda. I know I have you and Janette to thank for making her feel so settled.' She ushered them into the familiar lounge and automatically Magda sat down where she had always done, nodding at Max to join her on the squishy but comfortable settee, leaving the automated riser chair for Beth.

While Beth was in the kitchen making tea for the visitors, Magda told Max all about her former life. She found it easy suddenly, strangely to share that with her relatively new friend before Beth came bustling in with a tray, which Max jumped up and took from her.

'Allow me, dear lady.'

Magda could see that he was already charming her friend.

'Magda dear, I have news. A lovely young couple, not unlike you and dear Dennis have bought the flat upstairs. And, they have a lovely little Westie called Hamish whom they're going to let me take out into the garden for them while they're at work. I'm going to take the little fellow for a walk too.'

Magda was delighted that Beth was going to have good neighbours. 'Oh, Beth, I couldn't be more pleased for you. That is indeed news. Have they moved in?'

'No, not yet. Three weeks to go, apparently. Then I can finally say goodbye to that awful Mrs. Axelrod! Do you know she did nothing but complain! The bins, the rubbish she said was on the pavement, the noise... I'm so relieved they're going.'

Magda was too. For her there had always been a little residual feeling of guilt about leaving her friend, who had been so very kind to her.

Max meanwhile had spotted a photo of Arthur. 'Is that your late husband? My goodness what a fine fellow he was eh?'

Beth was delighted and went on to regale him with Arthur's exploits. Magda, having heard these stories many times before, sat back and contemplated her own memories and feelings.

After a couple of hours, several cups of tea and some lovely cheese and homemade chutney sandwiches, Magda told Max it was time to leave. 'It's the dogs you see, Beth. Janette has gone in to let them out, but I ought to get back to them soon.'

'Oh yes your delightful little dogs. Have you told Max who persuaded you to have them?'

'She has indeed, and I too am very enamoured of the little cricketers.' The remark made both Beth and Magda smile. As they passed each other in the hallway Beth squeezed Magda's hand.

'How was it?' she whispered.

'Actually, it was okay. I laid some flowers and I told him about my new life. I wanted him to know I was managing.'

Beth squeezed a bit tighter. 'That's what he'd want you know. You have to live your life now my dear. If someone else comes into it, they won't be taking Dennis' place. They will have been brought in to enrich you.'

Magda smiled at her friend. 'I know. I know Dennis would want me to be happy. I know if he had been the one left, that's what I would have wanted for him.'

They embraced, kissing each other on the cheek.

'Always lovely to see you dear Magda and don't be a stranger.'

Magda smiled and assured her friend she would visit again soon and Max delighted Beth by taking her hand and kissing it, before they left.

'What a lovely lady. She must have been such a comfort to you. You know, when it was needed, I mean.'

'Yes she was. I really don't know what I would have done if it hadn't been for Beth. I didn't really know her that well you see. Dennis and I were always so busy. We both worked full time and leisure time we spent together. She always asked us in for a sherry at Christmas and Easter, things like that. Arthur had died just before we moved in. That was when she had the house made into two flats. We were the first new occupiers.'

'And a lovely job they made of it too. Your upstairs flat must have had a magnificent view over the woods. It would have been like living in a nest.'

Magda laughed. She and Dennis had often remarked to that effect. Instead of making her feel sad, she felt happy knowing her new friend now shared something of her old life.

When they arrived home, Magda found a note on her kitchen table from Janette telling her she had taken the dogs out for a long walk so Magda made tea for herself and Max.

'Your air force chap shown up lately?' Max asked suddenly.

'Actually, yes. Funny you should ask. He knocked last night. He's such a strange man though. I was in bed and came down in my dressing gown. You'd think he'd never seen a woman in a dressing gown before. I invited him in, but he refused. He just said he was sorry to have disturbed me and left.'

'Always thought he sounded a bit of a rum fellow to be honest. If he comes again and acts strange, just point him in my direction. I'll soon give him what's what. You don't need anyone like that bothering you.'

Just then Janette arrived back with the dogs. 'Oh hello you two, you're back. These have had a lovely walk by the river. We met some strange man who recognised the dogs.'

Magda's heart began to beat faster, believing Janette meant Adrian.

'You know the one Magda. Lives in the cottage over the other side. Made a great fuss of these two and asked where you were.'

Magda breathed a sigh of relief. It was Tom! 'Oh, yes. I went to visit him once. He's a lovely old man.'

'Goodness Magda, Janette and I have lived here for years and here's you here five minutes and already you know more locals than we do.'

They all laughed at that.

'Yes, this one's a *femme fatale* all right. There's someone I know thinks so too.' When Magda looked puzzled, Janette said, 'Your boss of course. You must know he's really smitten with you.'

'Phil? Janette don't be silly; of course he's not.'

'I think you'll find he is. Don't worry though, he knows your circumstances. He won't jump on you or anything like that. I know he has a soft spot for you though.'

'Oh God, Janette; now I won't be able to face him. I'll feel so embarrassed.'

'Don't be daft. He's a real gentleman too just like our Max here.'

'Hey, I'm not above fancying the odd woman or two.'

'Yes, we know and they would have to be very odd indeed.'

Janette flashed a wicked smile at Max. Magda was still too shocked by the Phil thing to join in. Instead she went into the kitchen to make more tea.

Chapter Nineteen

IN the end they all ended up ordering a takeaway, Max went home to get a bottle of wine and Janette went to get dessert for them. The atmosphere was jovial as always and when Magda was eventually clearing up she reflected that, despite the day having its sad moments, it had been lovely; a day to remember and cherish.

She glanced at her watch and despite feeling tired, didn't want to get ready for bed, just in case Adrian turned up. It would, she found herself thinking, be the perfect end to the day. Gone were her feelings of anger about the previous evening. Magda knew he was different from all the other men she had known. There was something special about him and now she had visited Dennis and talked to him, she did feel that maybe she could move on. If so, then she admitted to herself, *Adrian might be the one.* It was a big admission and sent her into a bit of a tailspin but she knew she was being honest with herself at last. 'Sorry Dennis, I do hope you don't mind,' she whispered into the ether and hoped he was listening.

Funnily enough once she had made that decision, instead of feeling anxious and worried, she felt it was right. Everyone had said that Dennis would want her to be happy and deep down in her heart of hearts she knew he would. He had been such a kind and gentle man. He had loved her to bits just as she had him, so he would never want her to be sad. She recognised this now as the truth and so thinking of sharing something with someone else was not a bad thing.

Magda sat reading by the light of her little table lamp well on into the night, but nobody knocked on her door. Just after midnight she got up and let out the dogs.

As she waited for them to come back inside a flash of white caught her eye. It was there one minute and gone the next. *That has to have been a barn owl,* she thought as she called for the dogs to hurry up. They seemed bent on exploring every shrub and bush that were becoming tinged with frost. Finally, they gave up and scampered in, sitting down by the biscuit tin where they knew Magda kept their treats. Even Aymes seemed settled so Magda gave them a *Bonio* each and made another cup of tea, which she took up to bed. There was no work the following day, but she couldn't help thinking of what Janette had said about Phil. Surely, he couldn't have a thing for her. She began to feel so embarrassed. She liked her boss a lot and he had been very supportive of her. However, there was no trace of any emotional connection on her part, only an appreciation of him as a friendly boss. *Janette's got it all wrong*, she thought as she snuggled down into bed.

Frighteningly, the dream came almost immediately. She was running away and people were chasing after her. In the distance she could see the huge orange ball of fire that had been a plane, but she knew she wasn't safe until she got inside her home. The stones bit into her feet and her heart was pounding with adrenaline from the dangerous men shouting at her. If they caught her, she had no idea what they might do. She was aware of the long white dress she was wearing and could feel the weight of her hair on her shoulders and down her back.

'You can't hide from us, you German whore.' She could almost feel his breath on her neck as she ran.

'*Sono Italiana, non sono Tedesco,*' she panted out the words as she ran.

Suddenly she was inside her cottage but they were banging on her door and pounding at the windows. She heard the shattering of glass and then she was overwhelmed by the smell of burning. Shaking, she stood there not knowing what to do. Like a fool she had trapped herself inside. The smell got stronger and she watched in horror as a line of flames began to lick their way towards her. The smoke was overpowering and however many times she coughed she could not clear her lungs, or breathe in enough air.

'I love you' was her last thought as she succumbed to the smoke.

Magda woke with a start. That was the worst, most realistic dream she had ever had. She had lived it; felt the fear, the flames, the heat, everything. Gently she pulled up her tee shirt expecting to see burns but of course there was nothing there. Her skin was as smooth as ever. Warily, she climbed out of bed and padded into the bathroom to fill her tooth mug with cold water, and splash some on her face. She drank down all the cold liquid before returning to her bed. *I must be going mad* was her last thought as, worn out, she succumbed to sleep.

When she woke she was shocked to see it was almost nine thirty. She was surprised the dogs hadn't woken her. She felt so weary and heavy as she crawled out of bed. *That awful dream*, she thought as she wandered down the stairs and opened the back door for the dogs. She filled the kettle and put it on to boil.

Once she had had some coffee, she began to feel more human. She went to have a shower and get dressed. Looking in the mirror she felt scared that she would see that face behind her; that face that she seemed to know so well now. There was nothing there of course and once again she chided herself for being silly.

She got the leads and took the dogs for a walk.

On her way back she popped into the shop to pay the paper bill and Linda greeted her now like an old friend. 'Hello Magda, hold on I'll just get water for the dogs.' She disappeared into the back, returning with a bowl from which the dogs lapped greedily. 'Thank you so much for those lovely flowers. Well, I guessed they were from you. Jim really misses his mum you know, even though she had been in that home for a couple of years. She really took to you, you know.'

'She was a lovely lady. I can imagine how much your husband must miss her.'

Linda gasped and put her hand to her mouth. 'Oh sorry, me and my big mouth. You lost your husband, didn't you? So sorry. I didn't mean to bring up bad memories for you.'

'It's okay. It was awful for quite a time, but I realise what they mean when people say *Life goes on*. It does and somehow you are borne along with it!' Linda gave her arm a squeeze.

'You need to tell my Jim that.'

'Oh of course, if you think it would help.'

'Why don't you pop in for a cup of tea on Sunday afternoon? You could have a chat with Jim. Don't let on that I said anything to you mind. That would really get his goat.'

Promising to be discreet, Magda accepted the invitation.

Wednesday was the next day Magda had to go into work. She felt awkward and embarrassed. Janette's revelation made her wonder whether she should give up the job. There was nothing worse, in her eyes, than having to let someone down gently.

The weather was now really cold so Magda selected a silk shirt to wear with a long black woollen skirt and a long waterfall style cardigan. She didn't like wearing tights or stockings so instead chose buttery leather black boots to go with her outfit. She grabbed her coat, bag and brief case and went outside to meet Janette only to find her in a bad mood for once.

'So sick of having to take on all the deliberate self-harm shouts. We're in desperate need of another social worker. Megan went on maternity leave but she's extended it which really leaves me in the lurch.'

Magda, remembering how it had been in her old job, sympathised. 'Maybe they could advertise for a temp?'

'Yes, that's what I asked Rachel. I don't suppose you know anyone do you?'

Magda shook her head. She hated seeing Janette upset like this, but everyone she knew in the health service lived in London.

'I didn't think you would. To be honest we were so lucky to get Megan.'

There was a heavy silence as they motored on.

When they got to work, Magda found she was fully booked. She walked up to her office and Jenny and Ross greeted her warmly. They had quickly made friends and usually found themselves roaring with laughter about lots of silly things together.

'Hello Magda, did you see your list? You've got a busy day. We've allocated you to room two downstairs. Is that okay?'

'Yes, thanks, that's fine. How was everyone's weekend?'

'Seems a long time ago now, doesn't it, Jenny? These part timers.' Ross laughed and Magda pretended to throw something at him. Just then, much to her embarrassment, Phil walked in and Magda busied herself on her laptop. She actually jumped when she felt a touch on her arm.

'Magda, might I have a quick word? I don't think your first client is until ten,' and with that Phil turned to Jenny. 'Would you mind making a coffee for Magda only I need a word with her.'

Magda gulped. 'It's okay Jenny, I'll make one later.'

'It's no trouble Magda, I was just going down to make one for myself.'

Giving her a grateful smile, Magda rose and followed Phil out and into his office.

'Take a seat.' Phil removed some papers from the armchair and indicated for Magda to sit. He flashed her a smile but although she returned it, hers was rather tighter.

'How are you Magda?'

'Oh, I'm good thanks. How are you?'

'Very well, thanks. Now…'

The door pushed open and Jenny handed over Magda's mug.

'Thanks so much.'

Jenny winked as she left.

'Okay. Now you might be wondering why I wanted to see you. The thing is, we're all really impressed with your work and we wondered if you might consider increasing your hours? The funding's there if you wanted to.'

Magda was pretty sure she didn't want to, but felt badly about letting down the team. She knew, that as with Janette's team there were too few workers to cope with the influx of clients.

Sensing her hesitation, Phil smiled at her. 'Look you don't have to decide now. Think about it and let me know. I meant it though about how delighted we are with your work. You show such empathy for your clients and they are all positive about you I know.'

Magda was heartened by his comments. It almost made her say she would take the hours, but she managed to stop herself. She knew in her heart that three days were enough at this time, and of course, thanks to her Dennis and his insurance she didn't need the money.

On her way home she told Janette who was, of course, keen for her to take the hours. 'We must have had a windfall. Rachel has offered me a temporary replacement for Megan, for two days a week too. I just hope we can find someone.'

Magda hoped so too for her friend's sake. Janette was looking tired these days. She was sure after reflection that she did not want to take on more work herself. She had enough good days but there was still the odd bad one. She was too professional not to want to be able to be fully present for her clients during sessions and she determined that the following day she was going to speak to Phil and turn it down.

Anyway, the next thing was tea with Linda and Jim at the garage. Magda picked a bunch of late blooming roses which she wrapped in some paper and took with her. Magda was made to feel very welcome and there was a splendid assortment of cakes to go with the tea but Magda could feel the depth of Jim's sadness. She ignored all Linda's pointed looks and comments though as she felt Jim was not ready to hear what she might have to share. Instead she chose leaving as the best moment to whisper to him. 'It does get easier you know.'

It probably hadn't been enough for Linda, but Magda knew all too well, from first-hand experience that you had to be ready to move on and Jim was nowhere near that yet.

At work next day Sarah was her first client and Magda had thought she was coming on in leaps and bounds. Usually now she no longer looked and sounded anywhere near as timid. In fact, at one session she had delighted Magda by saying she thought if they hadn't been therapist and client, they would have been friends which Magda took as a great compliment.

Today though Sarah seemed back to her old self. She kept looking at the wall instead of meeting Magda's eye. She had been like that when they first began to work together. After a while she settled and began to say she had managed to cook Spaghetti Bolognese for dinner the other evening. Knowing that Leon, her ex-husband had once held her hand over the lighted ring had understandably made her as phobic about using the stove as his attempt to drown her had fuelled her fear of the bath.

'Oh, Sarah I'm delighted. How did it feel to make yourself a lovely hot dinner?'

'At first I was shaking but then I thought of you and our sessions together and I just kind of got on with it.' She gave a little smile and Magda returned it reassuringly.

They began to talk about Christmas, always a difficult time for a number of clients. 'I don't think Lucy will want to be with me.' Lucy was her teenage daughter.

'And how do you feel about that?' Sarah suddenly gasped and Magda almost jumped. 'Is everything okay?'

Sarah, obviously scared, failed to answer either question. Instead she burst into tears and began to sob out a long story about being able to sense and sometimes even see things. 'Magda is your mother alive? I know you shouldn't reveal personal details but I saw this lady standing behind you, so I wondered if your mum had passed and I was seeing her. Please don't have me sectioned though will you? I'm not mad, honestly.'

Magda reached out for Sarah's arm. Despite the cold shiver that had gone through her, her first thought was Sarah's welfare.

'Sarah, of course I don't think you're mad. I've got to know you over the weeks and although you've been through real trauma, you are still well grounded in reality and you're working through that trauma and doing brilliantly.'

Magda took a deep breath. She was unsure how to proceed. She was trained never to ignore or negate a client's feelings or beliefs. However, if Sarah *had* seen a reflection behind her, then surely it had to have come through the glass panel in the middle of the door. It couldn't be anything else. 'I think maybe you saw a reflection of something.' That was the best Magda could come up with. She knew it sounded lame but Sarah seemed to accept that, although several times during the rest of the session she seemed to be looking round for something with a puzzled little frown on her face.

For once Magda was not sorry to draw the session to a close. Telling Sarah how well she had done with the cooking and that they would meet at their usual time next week, she saw her to the door. She felt that she had dodged something Sarah had wanted to explore and she felt badly about it. Her worst fear was the possibility that the figure Sarah had seen could have been Maria!

When she returned to the office and opened her laptop to write up the notes, her hands were shaking so much that Jenny noticed. 'You okay Magda? Difficult session?' Jenny was used to therapists coming back, needing to offload. She was not just a brilliantly organised departmental secretary but a good listener too.

Magda tried to pull herself together. 'No, not really. It was Sarah and actually she's doing really well. I may just have drunk too much coffee.' She gave a laugh which she knew sounded false and hollow.

'Well that's good because I was just going to suggest we went downstairs and got a cup of tea!' Jenny handed Magda her mug. 'Come on, your next client isn't due yet.'

Together they walked down the stairs to the team room, with Jenny talking about her children. 'God, the things they know these days. Casey's eight going on nineteen! I don't know what to do with her sometimes. I caught her watching this really explicit pop video she said her Polish friend showed her. I told her she'd be banned from using the laptop if she kept looking at things like that! Mind you, her little friend has an older sister, so I guess that's where that came from. I'm luckier with Luke as all he wants to do is go fishing.'

Jenny's chatter was just what Magda needed to ground her. *It had to have been a reflection Sarah saw* she told herself sternly as they walked in to make their tea.

'Oh, there you are Magda, I've saved these for you,' Paul, the only male nurse in the team, called out. Magda had confessed to liking liquorice so he'd taken to saving the liquorice toffees from the bags the support workers bought each week. She thought it was really sweet.

'Thanks Paul.' She took the three he held out for her. Everyone here was just as lovely as Janette had promised her.

Chapter Twenty

THE rest of the day passed without incident apart from Phil asking if she had made her decision about the extra hours.

'I'm sorry, Phil. I should have come to find you, but today's been busy. I'm afraid I'm going to say no. I think what I have at the moment is just about right for me. At this time, I mean.' She couldn't help but notice the look of disappointment that came over his face.

'That's a real shame. As I said we're so pleased with your work. Your clients are coming along so well by all accounts. I understand though. Janette told me about your...er...bereavement.' He blushed bright red, fearing, Magda felt, that he had overstepped the mark.

'No, it's okay. It is about that in part. I still need the down time at the moment. You never know, if the funding's still there in a year or so then I could well be persuaded to take on more. Right now, I need the space too.'

'I get it. I really do. I won't appoint anyone else then, or maybe we could take on another student. We do that from time to time if they can hold a caseload.'

Magda thanked him for being so understanding.

On the way home Janette asked Magda if she had made any plans for Christmas.

'No, not at all. In fact, I haven't really considered it.' And then it hit her – the anniversary!

'Sorry, Magda. Didn't mean to bring up sad memories but I was wondering if you wanted to come to me for Christmas lunch? I'm staying put this year and visiting the baby in the New Year. I thought we saddos – you, me and Max - might find it fun spending the day together. However, if it's too soon, I'll understand.'

Magda couldn't stop the tears that came so easily at the thought of the holiday. Hastily wiping her eyes with a tissue she thanked Janette for her kind offer. 'In fact, I'd love to come for dinner. I'll bring things too; whatever you need. How about if I make dessert, or do you go for the traditional Christmas pudding?'

'Well yes, I do rather and brandy sauce. I make my own, pudding that is. It's all made already and maturing nicely. I use lots of brandy.' She winked at Magda. 'However, a lovely fruit salad would go down a treat for supper.'

'Have you asked Max?'

'Oh yes. Well, I didn't have to. It's a bit of a tradition since the last Mrs. Max left.'

Magda couldn't help but smile. They really did look out for each other, and it was lovely.

As usual Magda found Rollins waiting by the door for her and no sign of Aymes. She put down her bags and took off her coat. The house was lovely and warm thanks to the heating coming on an hour before she got home.

Aymes condescended to come down when he heard the food being spooned into his bowl and Magda pushed him outside before letting him eat. She made herself a cup of tea and contemplated dinner. An overwhelming feeling of tiredness came over her. So much so that she had to sit down at the kitchen table. *Perhaps it's to do with the anniversary coming up* she wondered as she sat there. *It's the first too.* She glanced over at the two little dogs munching away and a wave of love came over her together with one of gratitude to Beth for making her have them. She would be lost without their company, even with Janette and Max so close.

That evening she rang Beth. 'Oh, hello my dear. How strange. I was just about to call you. I was worried with Christmas on the horizon. I would have loved to have spent the holiday season with you, you do know that, but you remember my friend who had the heart attack? Well I'm going down to spend Christmas with her. I just wondered what you might be doing and will you be all right?'

Once again Magda's emotions were triggered. 'Thank you, Beth. I'm going to be fine. I'm going to spend the day with Janette and Max. We're all getting together at Janette's. I'm sure I'll be okay even though this isn't going to be the best of times for me. How is your friend doing?'

'Do you know, she's made a remarkable recovery and she's even going to the gym of all things! Apparently, they have some ancients' cardiac workshop thing. As long as she doesn't expect me to join her.'

Beth laughed and Magda joined in. They chatted for a while and Beth told Magda she thought she had made the right decision not to increase her working hours. For a second Magda contemplated telling her about Sarah and the session that morning. Something stopped her though. She didn't want Beth alarmed for her.

After dinner Magda sat there contemplating the upcoming anniversary. It was bound to be hard. A stray thought that she didn't really want, crept in – *Adrian!* She had seen no sign of him since the summer. He had just disappeared. At first, she had waited for him to arrive, but soon realised he was not coming back. *They must have transferred him to another base*, she had thought once a couple of months had gone by. She had felt rather hurt that he had not thought to come by and tell her, and say goodbye. However, he had been a real enigma so what could she expect! *Now I just have to get through this Christmas* she told herself. Of course, Christmas Eve was the actual anniversary and she had no memory of what she had done last Christmas Day and Boxing Day or indeed the days that followed. She had been prevented from making any funeral arrangements over the holiday period so there was a completely blank week or more before there were practical arrangements to address. Her in laws had eschewed her invitation to stay with her when they came over, preferring to book into a *Bed and Breakfast*. Now she was faced with the whole reality of it all over again.

For the intervening month she would just have to concentrate on work. This reminded her of Sarah and what she said she had seen or sensed. It could have been the spirit of Magda's mother of course but she and Magda hadn't been that close. It was her father with whom she had forged the stronger bond. *It was a shadow, it had to have been* she told herself yet again as she got ready for bed.

The month went by so quickly. Work was busy and one morning Phil came in and told them he had arranged for a student to come in January for some work experience. He winked across at Magda as he told them, letting her know she could increase her hours whenever she felt ready. There was a Christmas lunch for their team and a Christmas party for everyone. Magda told Janette she didn't mind driving that day so Janette could drink. She wasn't in a festive mood at all. In fact, she was dreading everything to do with the holidays. She had received lots of cards from friends of what she now thought of as her *old life* and dutifully she had sent cards back to them.

Then Max turned up one evening bearing a huge Christmas tree. 'Now I know just what you're going to say, but you need this and he needs you. Look it's got roots and everything. Once Christmas is over, we can plant him in the garden. Come on now you must have a bucket somewhere.'

Funnily enough she did have a large leather one that had belonged to her grandmother during the war. She had been a member of the Women's Land Army. The bucket had been presented to them at some ceremony or other. Her grandmother had been Polish and it was after her that she had been named Magdalena. Wearily sighing, she went to the shed to retrieve it.

'Here you go, but I don't have any decorations. I got rid of all mine when I moved.'

Max looked sly as he manoeuvred the huge tree inside. He left it in the utility room while he went to get some earth for the bucket.

Magda opened a bottle of wine and poured a glass for each of them. She felt she had to do something to show willing.

Max came striding back with the bucket and a smug look on his face. From a polythene bag he produced three strings of fairy lights and some silvered pine cones tied with red bows. Magda gasped. She could see the decorations were beautiful and tasteful and more than anything else they were the kind Dennis had always used to decorate their trees in the past. Almost against her will she began to help Max with the tree. They strung the white fairy lights around and around interspersing the branches with the cones. It looked beautiful and Max showed her that the lights were all battery operated. Gratefully he accepted the glass of wine and the two of them sat in the dark with just the glow of the gas fire and the fairy lights. It made the little room look magical.

'Penny for them?' Max nudged her. He could sense that she was sad.

'It's nothing. The tree is lovely, thank you. It's just that the decorations would be just the ones Dennis would have chosen.'

'You see! A man of impeccable taste is what I am.'

In the end Max invited Janette in to see their handiwork and they ended up ringing for a take away curry. They chatted about Christmas Day and what Janette would like them to bring for lunch and tea. They planned to spend the whole day there until late evening. Then gently Janette asked Magda if she would like to accompany her to a carol service on Christmas Eve.

'It's okay if you don't feel like it. I go every year and it's lovely. The kids have Christingle lights and there's nothing preachy about any of it. I know that's going to be a hard day for you, but if you fancy some company, I leave here about four. It's in the Abbey at Ramsey.'

'Can I think about it and let you know?'

'Yes of course you can.'

Magda got up and went over to give Janette a hug.

'Do you go Max?'

'Oh goodness me, no. They wouldn't allow an old atheist like me within their walls.'

Janette picked up a cushion and threw it at him. Eventually they all decided it was time for bed. As Magda turned off the tree lights she looked out of the window to see if she could spot Dennis's star.

'I loved you so much.' She whispered out into the night.

Chapter Twenty-One

GRADUALLY Christmas crept nearer. Work seemed to have rather a frantic atmosphere and the two support workers, whom Rachel called her *Angel*s as they went over and above their duties, decorated the team room and Jenny did the same to their office. Magda came in one Wednesday to find her desk swathed in tinsel and glittery cards put up on the wall. These, together with the cards staff and clients had sent, which Jenny had stuck to the wall gave the work station a very festive look. *Of course, Jenny doesn't know how I feel about this time or even what happened* Magda thought as she pasted a smile on her face and thanked her for making the desk and walls look so pretty.

'Magda, you're so popular. Look at all the cards and you've only been here since September.' Jenny enthused.

'I'll say and I hope you've got in on our Secret Santa.' Ross gave Jenny a wink.

'Ask Phil what he got last year,' Jenny laughed and then the two of them exploded with laughter.

'Oh, Ross that's not fair. I'll tell you. His Secret Santa gave him a bow tie for his willy.'

Magda had to smile at that. Janette had picked for her as the draw had happened on a day Magda didn't work. She had handed the sealed envelope to her so she knew she hadn't peeked. Magda when she got around to opening it found she had drawn Rachel. That wasn't too bad as she knew she loved bath bombs and things like that. In fact, Magda had found a really lovely little basket of products at the Christmas Market in Peterborough when she went there the previous week. The lady behind the stall had even wrapped it in pretty cellophane and tied it with a bow. It had been a little over the price limit that had been set, but Magda liked Rachel so hadn't minded the extra expense.

The fever pitch went up a notch on the day of the Christmas lunch and party. As promised Magda drove herself and Janette in. Both of them clutched their Secret Santa gifts to themselves as they negotiated the icy pavement. There had been quite a frost the previous evening. They were both dressed up too in party style clothes, which for Magda was a long black velvet skirt with a chiffon and velvet blouse. She had teamed these together, feeling they were festive-looking, and had paired them with her black leather boots. Janette was wearing a patterned dress and heels! She clutched on to Magda, swearing 'Never again' every time she nearly tripped over in them.

Phil was at the door when they got in.

'Hello ladies. Good to see you. Looking lovely too, am I allowed to say?' Sometimes he struggled with the political correctness required these days.

Both of them smiled and assured him he could. He was dressed in a smart suit with a bow tie. Magda had only ever seen him in casual wear before and she had to admit he looked good dressed up. She had ignored the remark Janette had made about his having a soft spot for her and once over that had treated him as she would any other colleague and boss.

There were clients to see until lunchtime. Magda's second was Sarah and she was gratified that she had not mentioned anything strange since the last episode.

'You'll never guess.' Sarah was the most animated Magda had seen her. 'Lucy's coming to Christmas lunch. She's bringing her dog. I hope she gets on with Jake.' Jake was the Staffie-cross Sarah had adopted when she had been given her new council home. She had felt lonely, and like Magda, had never had a dog before. However, Jake had found his way into her heart in much the same way!

'Have they met before?'

'No, that's the thing. Lucy said she'd like me to bring Jake to the gate so that Milo can sniff at him and then hopefully once they've met they could have a run round the garden together.'

'Well that's lovely, and I'm so glad Lucy wants to come to have lunch with you.'

When the session was over, Sarah delved into her capacious handbag. 'I brought you this, it's a crystal. You use them for healing and things. I wanted you to wear this so I had it mounted on a chain. It's Rose Quartz; it'll keep you safe.' She handed the beautifully gift-wrapped box to Magda. 'I hope you don't mind, or think it's a cheek or anything.'

Magda could sense that Sarah was anxious. 'Mind! How could I possibly mind? Thank you for such a thoughtful and generous gift.' Magda opened the box and extracted the beautiful pale crystal on its delicate silver chain. It was perfect. She got up and gave Sarah a hug. 'Thank you. Now I wish you the happiest and healthiest of Christmases and we will meet again in the New Year. I look forward to it.'

Sarah beamed as she hugged her. 'Well Magda it's down to you that I can cook the Christmas Dinner.'

'Actually no, Sarah, you've got that wrong. It's your hard work in our sessions that mean you can cook the Christmas Dinner and because you're such a brave lady. I've only been here supporting you. You're the one who's done all the hard work.'

They hugged again and Magda made her way back to the office. As she was walking up the stairs a thought hit her. *Why would Sarah say the pendant would keep her safe?* Shaking her head, she entered the office. Everyone was gathered there and Phil had opened a bottle of Champagne.

'Ah there you are Magda, come and join us. We always celebrate our year this way. We're delighted to have you in the team now.' With a beaming smile he handed a full plastic beaker to her. 'Sorry about the cup. We don't have any glasses and we didn't want to use our mugs.'

Everyone laughed.

'That's nice Magda. What is it?' Jenny had come over.

'It's a gift from one of my clients. Do I have to enter it into a book here? I always had to at my old job.'

'Yes, we're the same. It's to keep everyone safe, you know, bribes and things, not that you would. I'll just quickly do it for you.' Jenny hurried over to her desk.

Magda felt herself redden when Jenny took it from her.

'Wow this is beautiful. Which client? They must think a lot of you.'

'And why wouldn't they?' Magda became aware of Phil's hand in the small of her back, obviously emboldened by the champagne,

Magda thought *I must be careful. In no way do I want to lead him on.*

Jenny meanwhile had written something down in the book and now she fastened the necklace round Magda's neck. 'It's beautiful, so delicate too.'

'It was Sarah, you know Sarah Dean. The domestic violence case.'

'Oh, I remember her, a little mouse. Goodness she must have come along since I assessed her.' Phil was beaming now.

'She has. She's worked really hard.'

Magda extricated herself from him and sat down at her desk. 'I'm going to write up my notes before we go to lunch.' She hoped she sounded firm and in control.

Lunch turned out to be great fun. Magda found herself seated between Ross and Jenny and it seemed as if they laughed from start to finish of the meal. Ross told them stories that were so silly you just had to laugh. The atmosphere was festive and for those couple of hours Magda was able almost to forget what had happened the previous Christmas. Nobody had any clients booked in for the afternoon so when lunch was over, they sauntered back into the office and made themselves coffee and tea.

Phil came up behind Magda and put his arm around her. For a moment she stiffened but he whispered that he hoped she was having a good time and didn't feel too sad. She said nothing but tried to take the whole thing as a gesture of friendship and nothing more.

The party in the evening was less to Magda's taste. It was far too manic and raucous. Everyone seemed to be so loud. They all exchanged their Secret Santa presents and Magda was very touched when she opened hers. Inside were two framed beer mats bearing the name *Cottage Whippet* and pictures of whippets which really did look a bit like Aymes and Rollins. She had a feeling Janette must have drawn her in the Secret Santa!

Magda was relieved when around nine Janette came over and asked if she'd had enough and was ready to go?

'Yes, absolutely. Let's get our coats.'

Once in the car Janette heaved a long sigh. 'Sorry, I should have warned you they tend to get rather loud around this time of year. I hope it wasn't too much for you.'

Magda wanted to say it was, but her friend had been too kind for such brutal honesty. 'It's okay. Parties have never really been my thing. In fact, I didn't go to my work do last year and Dennis, being freelance, didn't have to go to anything. We usually took things easy and quietly over the Christmas break.' She marvelled to herself that she could talk openly about Christmases past. She had indeed come a long way this year.

The last few days before the start of the holiday just sped by. All Magda's clients were stable, so she had no worries about the long break. She would not be back at work until the second of January and the office shut the day before Christmas Eve. Paul came up with a handful of liquorice toffees on the last afternoon. He said 'I hope the holiday season's going to be okay for you.' That made her think that everyone knew what had happened to her last year but she was touched by his thoughtfulness. 'Don't forget, you owe me a pint. Have it in the New Year, yeah?'

He saluted as he left.

Chapter Twenty-Two

SO here it was, the day she had been dreading. Magda woke with a sense of something being very wrong and immediately the date sprang into her mind. Of course! Christmas Eve. At first all she wanted to do was burrow down in the bed and hide. The dogs though had other ideas and wanted their breakfast. Wearily as if she carried the weight of the whole world on her shoulders, Magda got up and shrugged on her dressing gown. She went downstairs and opened the back door. A white winter wonderland greeted her. In the night it had snowed heavily, covering everything in a blanket of white. The air was freezing and as she watched the two dogs relieve themselves on a nearby bush, steam rose from their urine! Hugging her dressing gown round her, Magda called them back in and quickly shut the back door.

'Brrrrr it's cold,' she told their two upturned faces as she opened a tin of dog food. She placed the food into their bowls and when she had laid them down on the floor went to the utility room to turn up the boiler. Everywhere was so quiet, it felt as if the whole world was holding its breath. Not a sound came from anywhere. It was so quiet Magda could even hear the gentle tick, tick of the clock timer on the boiler.

She went back into the kitchen and began to make coffee and toast. The little cottage was snug and warm against the outside onslaught of freezing weather. Magda listened for the sound of the paperboy, but it would seem he was not coming. She guessed the snow would be the reason and actually smiled to herself as she imagined Linda's reaction to *the boy*.

After breakfast she decided to have a lengthy soak. She had been given bubble bath by one of her clients so she went upstairs and ran a deep bath. As she looked out into the garden while she waited for the bath to fill, something in the corner caught her eye; a flash of red that was there one minute and gone the next! *How odd*, she thought unable to spot any footprints in the snow. It had been there though, that glimpse of something red. It wasn't just her imagination. So intent was she that she almost let the bath overflow, just catching it in time.

It was heavenly to sink into the luxuriously hot, scented water. Magda lay there and let her tears flow naturally so that they merged into the cooling bath water. *Dennis*, she thought as she pictured him in her mind; tall, and graceful; gently curling, jet-black hair and the bluest eyes she had ever seen; his face ruggedly handsome despite the long eyelashes that would have looked good on a woman; his voice, the gentle Irish brogue; the way his hair fell across his forehead into his eyes when he was working on an illustration, cups of coffee long forgotten, cooling at his side as he became absorbed in his work.

And the fun they had had together. Nothing had come between them, even Magda's reluctance to start a family during what was to be the last year of their marriage - Dennis, with his usual equable charm had understood her reasons. 'Someday soon though darlin' eh?'

He had nodded at her and she had agreed. 'Yes, someday soon.' A day that could now never arrive!

Aware that the water had cooled to an uncomfortable temperature brought Magda back to the present. Scrambling out of the bath, she grabbed a nicely toasted towel from the radiator and began to dry herself and her hair. She walked into the bedroom and realised she was avoiding looking out at the garden. She *had* seen that flash of red and it had not been a robin. Nothing that small. She reached for the hairdryer and plugged it in. Her hair which was long and thick took ages to dry but when at last it was, she scrunched it into a messy bun, securing it with a chopstick.

She found thick trousers and a warm cashmere sweater and put them on. Then she went downstairs and scrabbled in the utility room for her walking boots. She donned those and her thickest coat and called the dogs. Rollins raced in, knowing it was time for a walk. His brother though had vanished.

'Aymes, come on, walk time.' Magda shouted as she put on Rollins little waterproof coat. After a few minutes she felt cross. 'Come on Aymes, walk.' Weary and frustrated, she stomped out into the kitchen but the dog wasn't there. She knew instinctively that she would find him under her bed and she was right. He looked up at her with worried eyes.

'Come on we're going for a walk and to get the paper.' Aymes continued to look unblinkingly at her so she went downstairs to find some ham with which to tempt him from his hiding place. That did the trick and finally she was able to put on his coat and lead and the three of them set out into the frosty, snowy landscape.

Magda wound her angora scarf tightly round her neck and wished she owned a hat. Hats were just something she never wore.

The bushes and trees were laced with snow and the whole landscape looked breath-taking, but goodness it was cold. *It never got this cold in London*, she thought as they tramped through the thick snow.

She passed the postman who waved cheerily as he stomped his way along.

'Hello there. Hornbeams? Hang on.' He produced a small parcel which he handed to her. 'There you go love, Merry Christmas' and with that he was on his way again.

Magda turned over the parcel seeing the London postmark. *Beth!* Knowing her friend was leaving before Christmas Eve, Magda had posted a package to her the previous week. She put her present into the capacious pocket of her coat and tramped on.

When she reached the paper shop she saw Linda trying to heave a sack of coal round to the entrance. *Surely poor Linda shouldn't have to do this alone.* 'Hang on. Let me help you.'

Linda turned startled and dropped the bag. 'Oh it's you love. It's okay I'm used to it. This one's for Mr Masters and he gets cross if it isn't there waiting for him by the door. He drives his truck up see and then loads it on.'

Mr Masters, Magda remembered was a local farmer who rather thought of himself as Lord of the Manor. She and Linda exchanged a knowing smile as tying up the dogs, Magda went over to help.

'Don't tell me, that boy never come this morning? I'll just go in and have a word with Jim. Thank you though Magda love, for the help.'

Magda followed her inside.

'Jim, that boy never showed did 'e?'

Jim who was patiently trying to organise the papers for delivery, shook his head.

'Told you.' Linda turned to Magda with a triumphant look on her face. 'Bit of snow and he do think him's goin' to melt.'

Jim smiled and shook his head. He handed her paper to Magda. 'Here you go girl, Happy Christmas to you too. Here, give these to them lads of yours,' and he handed two *Jumbones* to Magda.

Thanking him and wishing him and Linda a Merry Christmas, Magda left the shop. She could hear Linda going on about *that boy* until she was out of earshot.

The dogs were shivering standing in the cold, so Magda unfastened their leads and they shot off trying to eat the snow as they ran. They chased around and around in circles, clearly relishing the fun.

'Mornin', young lady.'

Magda turned to see Tom standing behind her.

'Merry Christmas to 'ee an all.'

'Hello Tom, Merry Christmas to you too. How are you?'

'Oh, I be the same, you know how tis. Me arthritis playin' up in this weather. Looks pretty, mind, don't it?'

'It's beautiful.'

'Oooh aye, and we don't often get a white Christmas these days. Well you know where I am. Pop in and see me any time. Just going to fetch me paper.' And with that he went into the shop, no doubt to receive in his turn another diatribe about *that boy.*

Back at the cottage there was no sign of Max or Janette and obviously the Griffiths had chosen not to spend Christmas at their holiday home. Magda had already received a lovely card from Gemma saying she missed her and the dogs while Magda had got their Essex address from Janette and sent Gemma a card from herself and the boys.

Once inside Magda opened her gift from Beth. It was a lovely rose gold bracelet with a small heart charm that looked very much like a ruby. The whole thing looked old and Magda wondered if it had belonged to her friend or perhaps it had been a gift from Arthur. *It's beautiful* she thought as she fastened it onto her wrist. It was delicate and suited her.

The day, however, then seemed to stretch endlessly in front of her. She went into the kitchen and heated a cup of coffee left over from breakfast. She opened the paper to the crossword page and began to solve it. An hour later when she looked at her watch it was still only half past ten!

Trying valiantly not to dwell on the previous Christmas Eve, she went upstairs to clean the bathroom but the thoughts kept intruding. *This time last year I was…and Dennis was still alive*, she kept thinking. He would have been reading the paper and then preparing to go out. There was something he said he'd forgotten to tell her, something important. Now she would never know what that something had been.

Magda remembered the little sad polythene bag of possessions, Karen the police lady handed to her, apologetically, it had seemed. Magda still had his wallet. She kept it in the bedside drawer.

With the bathroom spotless, Magda tackled the bed, changing the sheets and duvet cover.

Running out of chores she went back downstairs. The dogs were curled up in their basket in front of the gas fire. Magda sighed and sat down with a book.

Just then there was a tap on the window. Getting up Magda found Max standing there with a sprig of Mistletoe. She felt a little jolt of pleasure and signed to indicate he should come round to the back door.

Once inside Max divested himself of his huge overcoat and draped it over a chair. Smiling, his eyes indicated the Mistletoe he was holding over his head.

'Okay you win.' Magda walked over and kissed Max soundly. It was quite nice which rather surprised her. 'Coffee?' She asked once she had regained her composure.

'Please, good and strong.'

'Why? Heavy night?'

'God no, heavy nights are behind me. Just fancy one of your lovely strong Italian coffees. Then I'm off to find Janette; see her reaction to this.' He indicated the Mistletoe now lying on the kitchen table. Magda had to smile. He was such a flirt.

'By the way what happened to your air force chap? Don't hear anything about him these days.'

'Oh, I think he left. That is to say I haven't seen him for months.'

Magda smothered the feeling of sadness this added to her already overloaded mind.

Max continued. 'As I've said before, a bit of a rum sort Janette and I thought. We were quite worried about you to be honest. You were in a pretty vulnerable state.' He took her hand and squeezed it. Magda knew he meant well.

They sat drinking their coffee in amicable silence, both it would seem absorbed in their own thoughts. Magda wondered then about Max. He always seemed cheerful, but three failed marriages! Surely there had to be some residual sadness there. It made her think she was not the only one liable to be troubled on what was meant to be a happy day.

Coffee drunk, Max stood up to leave. 'I'll see you tomorrow then at Janette's.'

Suddenly there was an awkwardness about them that had not been there before. Magda smiled hesitantly but Max took hold of her hand again.

'I know how difficult today must be for you. I don't know what to say really. I'm at a faculty thing this afternoon; ghastly affair, tea and mince pies with the Dean, otherwise I'd ask you to come. That is if you wanted to. I'll be home around seven I guess although in this weather who knows! Janette's at home though you know, until she goes to that church thing. Are you going with her?'

'Honestly Max, it's okay. You don't have to babysit me the pair of you. No, I don't fancy going with Janette. I'll be okay here for the rest of the day. I've got the dogs and my book. I'll see if there's anything interesting on telly. I'm going to be fine; I have to be. Yes, this is the first anniversary and probably the worst, but I'll have to bear it. You go and enjoy mince pies with the Dean.'

Max grimaced then laughed. 'If I didn't love you as much as I do, I'd make you come with me.' With that parting shot he donned his coat and went off in search of Janette.

Just as she was preparing lunch the phone rang. She hesitated for a moment but then something made her answer it.

'Hello, dear. How are you? How are you doing? Have you got snow? We have.'

Magda's spirits cheered at the sound of Beth's voice. 'I'm okay thank you and yes we have snow; a lot of snow. How are you? And how's your friend?'

'We're fine thank you dear. Elsie's just come back from the gym. We're going to have some lunch, but I wanted to check you were feeling okay.'

Magda felt warmth spread through her. She was not really alone. Max had been, now it was Beth and no doubt Janette would check up on her at some time. Before they said goodbye Magda thanked Beth for her lovely gift.

'Oh you naughty girl. You weren't supposed to open that until tomorrow. Never mind, I'm just glad you like it.'

'Actually, I love it.' Magda held up her wrist and the delicate bracelet seemed to glow in the light.

'I hope you don't mind but it isn't new. In fact, it's the first thing my Arthur ever gave me. I can't take it with me but I can hope to bring some joy to you with it.'

Magda's eyes filled with tears. 'Oh Beth are you sure? I know how much you loved Arthur.'

'Of course I'm sure and yes I did, very much. I have all my memories of him to keep. I don't need to keep that bracelet and somehow when I looked at it the other day it reminded me of you. Now you wear it in health as they say.'

Thanking Beth once again Magda replaced the receiver.

As she had thought would happen, Janette knocked just after lunch.

'How are you? Did that rascal Max catch you with his Mistletoe?'

'I'm doing okay thanks, and yes he did.' Magda felt herself blush as she remembered the reaction she had had to his kiss.

'I wanted to ask about the carol service. With this weather I'm not sure I should go. However, if you really want to then we should make an early start.'

'Oh no, no. I wasn't going to come. Why is it snowing again?'

'Haven't you looked outside?'

Magda walked over to the window. The light was dim for two in the afternoon and huge white snowflakes were wafting down onto the already snow packed garden. The wind was whirling them around too. It looked beautiful in the silvery glow but not the kind of weather you would want to venture out in.

'What about Max? Isn't he going to some kind of thing with the Dean?'

'Yes, well he was meant to, but apparently it's been cancelled due to the weather. So how about we all have a pre-Christmas meal at mine?'

'Oh no! that's not fair, when you're cooking for us tomorrow. Let's have it here. I've got lots of food in.'

'Well you don't have to twist my arm. I'll let Max know. What time do you want us?'

'Say seven thirty?'

'Brilliant. See you then. We'll bring the wine.' With that Janette bustled out.

Magda thought having to entertain Max and Janette would do her good; stop her dwelling on last year. She decided to make a vegetable bake. She prepared all the vegetables and then got the dogs' leads.

'Come on boys, quick walk out in the snow.' This time both dogs materialised straight away.

It was absolutely freezing outside; the kind of cold that took your breath away. Snow was falling thick and fast so she decided to walk only a little way. Near the river she took off the dogs' leads and let them have a run round. Blowing on her hands because even with her gloves on they felt frozen, she began to stamp her frozen feet. She wondered then about Tom. Was he safely in that little cottage? She hoped he had enough food. There had been such an obvious lack of a woman's touch when she had visited him. Finally, the dogs had had enough and came bounding back. Rollins was busy trying to eat snow while Aymes ran round him in circles. Magda grabbed them and attached their leads. As they walked back to the cottage, it was snowing so hard the visibility was almost nil.

Once inside Magda gave the dogs a treat and began to prepare the vegetable bake but no sooner had she got it into the oven than the lights went out. *Oh no!* she thought. *Not a power cut.* But it was.

Luckily the oven was gas but she didn't relish the thought of entertaining in the dark. She rummaged around in the cupboard under the sink in search of some candles she remembered putting in there when she first moved in. Her hand closed round the packet and she brought it out. She remembered a candle stick in another cupboard but it took her a few minutes in the dark, to locate it. Then she had to find the matches before she could light it.

It was rather lovely to see the kitchen by wavering candlelight. Maybe dining this way wouldn't be so bad. Magda went into the lounge and lit the gas fire. They would need to eat with trays on their laps as this would be the only warm room once the heating died down.

With several candles now lit, Magda went upstairs to get changed. As she glanced out of the window, she could have sworn something was moving around outside. Has to be an animal, she told herself sternly. If so then I hope it's alright and can find somewhere warm to shelter. She couldn't bear to think of anything alone out there in the freezing weather.

Chapter Twenty-Three

AN hour and a half later and Magda had the lounge feeling cosy. The glow of the fake wood burner and the candles dotted around made it a welcoming place to be and a softly lit one by the time the first of her guests arrived.

'Brrrrrrrr I'm freezing my you know what's off, let me in.' There was Max in a huge black overcoat with a tartan scarf round his neck. *Goodness me*, she thought, *he's only had to come from next door.*

'Oh you wuss, come on in.' Magda held the door wide for him to enter. He was carrying what looked like a bottle of Champagne in one hand and a large Poinsettia in the other.

'Merry Christmas. These are for you.'

'Oh Max, thank you. Let me take your coat. Is it still snowing?'

'You bet it is.' Max shrugged off his coat and unwound his scarf. 'Janette'll be along shortly. She's just chatting to her son at the moment.'

Magda succumbed to Max's kiss on the cheek as she relieved him of his coat.

'What the devil's going on in here? What's with the candles? Not planning to seduce me are you? That might be awkward in front of Janette.'

Magda laughed. 'No, the power's off. It must be in your house too.'

'Yes of course it is but goodness me girl, you've got the generator! I said to Janette we were lucky to be here tonight at yours with that going.' Magda had completely forgotten about the generator.

Rapidly Max got back into his coat and scarf. 'Where's your torch.'

Thankfully Magda remembered exactly where she had put the large torch she had bought weeks before while shopping in Peterborough. 'Here.'

She handed it to him and taking it, Max stamped outside and she watched as he made his way over to the little shed. A minute or two later there was a humming sound and the lights in the cottage all came back on so Magda walked round blowing out the candles. She left the gas fire on but heard the gurgle of the central heating start up. *I can always switch the fire off if we get too warm* she thought as she set about laying the table in the kitchen.

Max came stamping back through the back door. 'That's better.' He gave a satisfied grunt as he looked around the lighted room. Helping him off with his coat, Magda hung it up in the utility room as Max took off his wellingtons. She felt rather embarrassed seeing his socks. It felt rather intimate, somehow, making Max look vulnerable.

Just then the back door opened to reveal what looked like the Abominable Snowman. 'Oh my, it's coming down thick and fast out there.' Janette spluttered as she handed Magda a bottle of wine and a box of chocolates. 'Blimey thank goodness none of us have to go anywhere. I wouldn't fancy my chances in that. I see you got the generator going. Well done.'

'Actually, it was Max.'

'Yes, silly girl had forgotten all about it. There was us thinking we could come here for light and warmth only to find her sitting in candlelight.'

Magda smiled as she flicked a tea towel at him and soon they were all sitting at her kitchen table with food and wine in front of them.

'Magda love, if the power hasn't been restored by tomorrow, how would you feel about my cooking our dinner here? I could come around nine and get everything going.'

'Oh Janette of course, that would be fine. I could give you a hand too.'

With that settled they all tucked into their meal.

'Mmmm, Magda this is nice.' Max was forking mouthfuls in as he talked. 'Bloody good thing the Dean's bash was cancelled. He made some mumblings about having it at New Year, but thank God I'll be away then.'

'Oh, are you going away then?' Magda realised she felt a bit put out that she hadn't known.

'Yes, darling girl. Off to Prague. Just for a few days over New Year, coming back the fourth of January.'

Janette it would seem had already had prior notice. Certainly she looked unsurprised.

Magda hadn't made anything for dessert but she had ice cream in the freezer and Max insisted they open the Champagne. 'A toast, to friends old and new.' He held his glass aloft looking at Magda. 'Family really should I say?'

Janette nodded her approval and Magda found herself blushing. Yes, they did feel like a little family all cosied up together eating in her lovely warm home.

Then old Tom sprang into her mind. 'Janette, you know that man who lives in one of the cottages over the river?'

'Old boy, goes down to the garage to get his newspaper?'

'Yes, that's the one. He invited me over there back in the summer. Poor man lost his wife. I was wondering. Do you think we should ask him if he wants to come tomorrow for Christmas dinner?'

Max gave a snort of laughter. 'Magda, you and your lame ducks.'

'What lame ducks?'

'Well that lovely lady who used to live below you and now this old boy who lives across the river. Where will it end?'

Magda knew he was only teasing but felt herself go on the defensive. 'If you mean Beth, she isn't a *lame duck* as you call them. She was the one who kept me going when Dennis died. If it wasn't for Beth making me adopt the dogs, then I wouldn't be living here now.' Overwrought, she felt tears spring into her eyes.

'Oh Magda, come on I was only joking. I think what you do for people is wonderful and you have such a big heart. You mustn't take offence, really, I was joking.' Max sprang up to give her a hug. 'Darling, I know this is a bad time for you. I was trying to make you laugh.'

Janette handed her a tissue as Magda succumbed and sobbed.

When she felt able to, she began to answer Max. 'No, please, please, I am so sorry. I know you were joking Max and I shouldn't have reacted like that. Honestly, I don't know what I would have done without you and Janette. Really, I would probably have stayed in bed all day today. You've made this day lovely instead of sad. Thank you both so much and I mean that.'

Max continued to hug her, while Janette patted her hand.

'We know, lovey and we're just pleased to be here for you. Goodness we agonised over who might buy Mrs Grigson's place and when you arrived it was like a breath of fresh air. We're just glad to be spending tonight here eating lovely food and enjoying ourselves. Now who'd like coffee?' Janette stood up and went to fill the kettle. Turning back to Magda she smiled. 'Now where exactly does this old man live? And Max will go round there in the morning and ask if he wants to join us, okay?'

'Okay.' Magda nodded a watery smile. 'There's one cottage on its own just as you go across the bridge. It's got a red door and there's Virginia Creeper on the walls. Oh, but that will have died back by now. It's the first cottage you come to.'

Magda didn't know why but she felt so saddened by the thought of Tom having to spend Christmas alone. She was sure too that Max didn't really want to go and get him. 'Look why don't I go. I know where he is.'

Magda did not miss the look Janette gave to Max who said 'No, no, let me. Honestly, I don't mind. I'm more than happy to rock up at a complete stranger's door and ask him over for Christmas Lunch.' The smile and wink he gave her though, showed he was still joking.

With that settled they took their Champagne, coffee and the box of chocolates into the lounge.

'Oh, by the way Janette do you have a bright red coat?' Magda asked remembering the flash of red she had seen earlier in the garden.

'No, not red. I do have a black and a tweed one. Why?'

'Oh, it's nothing. Just I thought I saw someone in the garden this morning wearing a bright red coat.'

'Postman?'

'No, it wasn't him. I met him later and he gave me some mail.'

'Not me either.' Max helped himself to another chocolate. 'I used to have a red jacket when those awful coloured ones were all the rage. Gave it to a charity shop though when I saw sense.'

This made them all laugh.

A couple of hours later they decided to call it a night. Before he went home, Max went out to the shed to top up the generator. There was still no sign of the power being back on.

'Have you reported it?' Janette asked Max.

'Oh no. I thought you would have.'

'I thought the same, thought you had.' Janette laughed. 'We'd better do it now.' She took her phone out of her pocket and scrolled down. When she had found the number, she went through into the kitchen where the signal was stronger.

She came back with good news. 'It's okay they already know. They hope to have us on by around eight tomorrow morning, all being well.'

Magda felt a pang of sadness that Janette wouldn't need to make the meal at her home. She had rather liked the idea of them working together in her kitchen. With it all settled the others departed, leaving her alone. Before they left, Janette had insisted on helping Magda to clear up so all she had to do was put on the dishwasher and get herself ready for bed.

When she let the dogs out, she was surprised to see it was still snowing heavily. There was not a sound and the whole garden sat still under its winter blanket. It was too snowy to be able to see any stars and Magda wondered where Dennis's star was hiding behind its blanket of cloud. 'Merry Christmas Dennis.' She whispered before calling the dogs back inside.

Magda woke the next morning to the green light of her alarm clock flashing and knew the power had been restored. She put on a coat over her nightclothes, put on her wellingtons and went out to turn off the generator. When she got to the shed she realised it was already off. *Oh bless him. Max,* she thought. *He must have beaten me to it.*

The snow had stopped but it was inches thick on the ground. She laughed at the two yellow trails where the dogs had spent a penny. Stamping the snow off her boots, she walked back inside. Of course, all the clocks needed setting again so she sorted that and then she made herself some porridge. The heating hadn't come on as the clock on the timer had stopped with the power cut so she went into the utility room to reset it. She was relieved when the boiler gave a hiss and the green light blinked on. Still huddled in her coat, she ate her breakfast and by the time she had finished the room was warming up nicely again.

After breakfast she set off for her usual walk with the dogs. She wondered what time Max would go and knock for Tom. *I should have done it,* she thought as she clumped on through the thick snow. The dogs of course, were enjoying themselves rushing around in the snow while trying to eat it. When she could stand the cold no longer she called them and they went home. Her phone was ringing as she came in.

It was an old work colleague who Magda hadn't heard from her in a while.

'Hello love, just wanted to see how you were and how things were going?'

'Polly, it's so lovely to hear from you. Yes, everything's going well thanks. How about you?'

'Oh, work is still the same. Nothing much changes. I'm determined to come and pay you a visit in the summer, if you'll have me of course.' She gave a chuckle.

'Of course, I will. It would be brilliant. Come and stay.'

'I'll take you up on that. Wouldn't mind a week in the sticks and I love Cambridge and Ely. We could go and visit both. It'll be fun.' They chatted together for a while before Polly said she had to go and begin the Christmas Dinner.

'Is Lorcan with you?' Lorcan was Polly's adult son.

'Oh yes, he's here great big lump. Not doing anything to help his poor old mum. And guess what? A girlfriend celebrating her birthday today with us too. I think this one might stick.'

'That's great. Give my love to Lorcan.' Magda had always had a soft spot for Polly's rather nerdy son. She was so glad he had found someone. So far he had been rather unlucky in love.

At Midday, bearing a freshly made fruit salad and a tiramisu cheesecake Magda knocked on Janette's door and Janette opened it with a flourish.

'Come on in, come in, Merry Christmas' She enveloped Magda in an enormous hug. 'Oh, thank you, these will go down a treat later I'm sure. I'll pop the fruit salad in the fridge, but do you mind if I freeze the cheesecake. I'm hoping you and Max will come to lunch or dinner tomorrow too, so that we can eat up all the leftover turkey. I think I went overboard on size this year. That cheesecake would be great for dessert then.'

'Of course.'

Shyly Magda handed Janette a beautifully wrapped present. She had agonised over what to get for her new friend and in the end had come up with a digital photo frame. That way Janette could put on all her favourite photos of Rose.

'Bless you. Take that in and put it under the tree. You'll find one for you under there somewhere.'

Magda did as she was told. Janette had made the lounge look very festive with her Christmas tree, bunches of holly and her cards all strung up along the ceiling beam. Under the tree was a pile of gifts. Some of them, Magda noticed, were for Janette's son, daughter in law and the baby. That reminded her that Janette was leaving for Brighton the day after tomorrow and Max would be going away too. Once again Magda would find herself alone in the little enclave. She couldn't help the shiver that ran down her spine at the thought. *Don't be ridiculous*, she told herself firmly as Janette came in to hand her a glass of sherry.

'I know, it's a bit of an old ladies' drink but I love a dry sherry at Christmas. It's almost tradition.'

Magda smiled as she sipped her drink. 'I agree. It must be years since I drank sherry. This one is lovely though, thank you.'

'Very welcome. Magda what did you and Dennis used to do on Christmas Day? Did you visit his parents?'

'Oh gosh no. I never met his father. He died before Dennis and I met. His mother though - she hated me. She was furious that Dennis married a non-Catholic. Poor Dennis bore the brunt of it all. He used to go and visit her on his own, as she told him I wasn't welcome in her home!'

'You're joking?'

'No, honestly. You should have seen her and his sister at the funeral. They stood as far away from me as possible. Never even gave me their condolences. So no, we didn't go to them at Christmas. Actually, we used to spend the holiday alone. We would go for a walk in the morning and then I'd make Christmas lunch. Dennis would help and then after lunch we would cuddle up on the settee and watch DVDs. It was heavenly to be honest. Just the two of us, nothing and nobody to worry about; such good times.'

Magda found to her surprise that instead of crying she was smiling at the thought of Christmases past. 'I was lucky.' She told Janette, who held up her glass.

'Here's to Dennis. I hope he knows I'm looking after you.'

'To Dennis and I'm sure wherever he is he does.' They were interrupted then by a knock at the door. A blast of icy air ushered in Max.

'Hello ladies, Merry Christmas. Now before we start, I went across to that old boy. I found the house and everything. Anyway, seems he's spending the day with a mate. Someone he knows from years ago, apparently. He was very touched though Magda, by your thinking of him. He sent you this. It's plum brandy that he made himself.'

Max handed over a rather dusty looking bottle.

'He said it'll put hairs on your chest, by the way.' Max took off his coat, put down the carrier bag he had been holding and gratefully accepted a glass of sherry from Janette. 'Here's to us.' He raised his glass and Magda and Janette followed suit.

The meal, when it arrived, was amazing and both Magda and Max congratulated Janette on her skills. Totally replete they all sat back once they had finished and Max suggested Magda open the plum brandy. 'Come along we may as well be together when we see that hairy chest.'

Magda took a mock swipe at him. 'I think we may have drunk enough.'

'Never, dear girl, never.'

Magda found the bottle and handed it to Janette to open. It smelled very strong and erring on the side of caution, Janette poured three small glasses.

'Here's to friends and family, absent and present.' Janette raised her glass in a toast, winking at Magda as she did so. 'My goodness.' With watering eyes, she advised the other two to take small sips. 'I'm not sure about hairs on your chest but this could strip paint.'

Magda took a cautious sip. It was delicious but exceedingly strong.

Janette, refusing Magda's offer of help to clear up, suggested they all go into the lounge to sit down. 'It might be a case of sit down before I fall down.'

Max was laughing, he had downed his glass of plum brandy and was now onto his second.

'Present time I think.' Janette walked over to the Christmas tree. She handed a parcel to Magda. It was heavy and when she opened it she found it contained an engraving of two dogs who looked very like Aymes and Rollins. 'I couldn't resist.' Janette laughed as Magda went over to hug her.

Magda handed hers to Janette. Her reaction was sheer pleasure. 'Magda that's stunning, thank you so much. I can put all the photos of the baby on it as she grows up.' Magda received her hug and couldn't help but notice that now there were tears in Janette's eyes.

'Come now ladies, there's still me to come.'

Janette rolled her eyes at Magda. 'Here you go, you annoying man.' She handed a parcel to Max who, looking like an excited but overgrown schoolboy tore it open. Inside was a first edition of an English history book from the previous century.

'Janette, you have outdone yourself. This is amazing. Thank you so much. Where did you find it?'

'In Brighton in a second hand bookshop.'

Max handed the book to Magda for her inspection. It looked heavy and dense to her, but she could see how much it meant to Max. She felt her gift would pale by comparison but she had done her best. She had bought him an old print of a cricket match, played out on some pitch far away years ago. He was gratifyingly appreciative. 'Truly amazing. I used to play you know, in my college days. Come here you angel and let me hug you.'

'I knew because you recognised Aymes' and Rollins' names, when you first met us.'

'Ah yes the delightful little cricketers. Where are they?'

'At home.'

'Well I think you should go and get them and let them enjoy some turkey.'

Janette nodded her agreement.

'Hold on though before you go, this is for you.' Max said.

She was careful as she took off the wrapping paper and inside found a little black box. When she opened it there was a silver bracelet with a dog's head charm. The head was an Italian Greyhound. Now it was Magda's turn to feel tearful. Throwing her arms round Max she kissed him soundly on the cheek. 'I *love* it, thank you so, so much.'

Grabbing her coat she went to get the dogs. Outside it was freezing cold. The snow crackled thickly under her ballet pumps. *Not the ideal shoes for this weather* she thought as she put the key in her front door. Standing inside, Magda had the strangest feeling that she was not alone. She couldn't explain it. There seemed a disturbance in the very atmosphere.

Almost holding her breath, she went in search of the dogs. Rollins was curled up in his bed by the radiator but not his brother. Feeling almost fearful at the thought of going upstairs, Magda approached her bedroom gingerly. Of course, only Aymes was there hiding under her bed. This time he came when called and tentatively wagged his tail.

'Come on you two, we're going to go and have some turkey!'

Probably due to the amount she had drunk, Magda did not retain any detail of the evening that followed. All she knew was that the three of them had a brilliant time. At around eleven, Max suggested he and Magda go home. She was warm and cosy but knew the trip out into the cold was inevitable. Thanking Janette profusely they wove their way home together with the dogs racing along in front. At her door Max gave her a warm hug and a kiss.

'Night, night Magda my sweet. I do hope your first Christmas without your man has been bearable.'

'Oh Max, more than just bearable it's been amazing. Thank you so much.'

With another hug, they parted, leaving Magda and the dogs to go inside. The house felt warm and Magda made herself drink a full glass of water. She didn't want to feel hungover in the morning, but knew she had drunk more than usual for her. She gave the dogs a *Bonio* each and then made tea to take up to bed. 'Night, night Dennis, Merry Christmas,' was the last thing she said as she sunk into a deep sleep.

As arranged the three of them spent the next day together. There seemed an awful lot of turkey left even after they had consumed some for lunch and had turkey sandwiches for tea.

'Magda take it home for the dogs, please do. I'm off tomorrow and I don't want to come home to it!'

Carrying the carcass in a polythene bag Magda kissed Janette goodbye and wished her a safe journey and a lovely time with her little grand-daughter. Max was off too, the day after, and already Magda was starting to feel bereft.

Chapter Twenty-Four

THE days between Christmas and New Year seemed endless to Magda, she missed Janette and Max so much. Janette had sent her a text to say she had arrived safely in Brighton and Magda had waved Max off at the door as the taxi taking him to the airport bore him away. She busied herself doing things in the cottage, walking the dogs and reading. She wished at times that she had not taken leave from work. She could have gone in as usual.

Gradually the snow began to thaw and by December the thirty-first it had largely cleared. Beth rang Magda to wish her a happy New Year and said she was back home so they agreed a date for Magda to come to fetch her to come and stay for a long weekend. Life it seemed would settle down into its comfortable groove after the holidays.

'I'm longing to meet your friend Janette, and to see that lovely Max again. So, what do you think the last weekend in January, weather permitting?'

'Lovely. I can come for you Saturday morning then take you back Monday afternoon.'

'Well I am quite the gadabout these days.' Beth laughed.

Magda wandered over to the window and was surprised to see it had started to snow again. She didn't stay up to midnight, not seeing the point of doing so. Instead she went to bed with a cup of tea and a box set to watch.

Her friends though had other ideas. First Max rang from Prague to wish her Happy New Year, disconnecting only to be replaced on the line by Janette. This call was closely followed by Polly and then finally Ross who was round at Jenny's celebrating.

'Come, Magda, why don't you get in your car and come over?'

Magda could tell that a lot of celebrating had already taken place. 'That's lovely of you, but no, not tonight. I tell you what, how about you and Jenny coming over for a meal in the New Year?'

'Oh yes, that would be great, wouldn't it, Jen?'

Magda could hear Jenny's enthusiastic response in the background.

'That's settled then. We'll fix a date when we get back to work.'

Lying back in bed Magda reflected yet again on how lucky she had been. *Moving here was the best thing I could have done* she thought to herself, as she snuggled down with the dogs under the duvet. She must have dozed off to sleep as she woke with a start to find the DVD had finished and looking at her clock she saw it was gone three. She got up and turned off the television. Parting the curtains, she saw that once again the whole garden was a whiteout and that snow was still falling heavily. Scrambling back to bed, Magda snuggled down again and it was not long before sleep reclaimed her.

New Year's Day was another quiet one. Magda walked the dogs and spent the rest of the day in the warm alternating reading with watching films.

At around eight thirty the lights dimmed and then went out completely. *Oh god no! Another power cut,* Magda thought as she went into the kitchen in search of the torch. *Dare she start the generator?* She waited a little while but with the heating going off the cold began to creep over her and she knew she would have to.

I wish Max was here, she thought before telling herself sternly that she must not begin to rely on him every time she needed help. Scrabbling in her bag she found her mobile and on it the stored number Janette had given her for the electricity company. She dialled the number only to get an automated voice stating that they were aware of the situation and hoped to have power restored to the area by midday the following day.

Oh no! Magda thought, *that's too long to wait. I'm going to have to start the generator.* Pulling on her wellingtons and coat she grabbed the torch and went out into the garden. There wasn't a sound to be heard. The whole atmosphere was eerily quiet and white. Everywhere was covered in the thickest of white blankets and snow was still falling heavily, if anything heavier than it had at Christmas.

Gingerly Magda picked her way over to the shed. At first, she couldn't get the door open and she wondered if the lock was frozen. Then after she gave it a good shove the door opened and she almost fell inside. Righting herself she shone the torch on the generator that squatted there like a malevolent creature from another planet. *Go on,* she told herself firmly, *Max got it going easily.* Trying to remember his instructions she peered into the tank that held the fuel, noting that it looked almost full. She found the lever easily enough. *Here goes nothing,* she thought as she gave it a big pull. There was a humming sound and the light on top flickered orange.

Breathing a huge sigh of relief, Magda bid a hasty retreat from the little shed. She crunched across the garden and stamped the snow off her boots before going indoors. Inside the lights were on and she could hear the ticking of the radiators beginning to heat up. She let the dogs out for the final time and then went on up to bed.

Magda felt strangely tired considering how little she had been doing over the past few days. She flicked on the television and settled down to watch.

After an hour or so her eyes began to droop so she made herself get up to clean her teeth. With that done she turned off the television and lay down once again, this time to go to sleep.

At some point in the night a huge bang seeped into her consciousness but she was so drowsy she couldn't even find the energy to rouse herself. Instead she turned over.

Suddenly she became aware that she was having trouble breathing. As she tried to sit up it was if a hand was pushing her down. Panic stricken, she fought her way into a sitting position and was horrified to find her room filled with black smoke. *It's a dream*, she told herself, *just like before*. About to lie down again she heard a crackling noise and to her terror a line of orange flames appeared under the bedroom door. It was no dream.

She tried to jump out of bed. The smoke though was pushing her back and she had to fight her way to the bedroom door. Breathing as lightly as she could she gave the door a push and was engulfed in a wall of orange flame. With one last heave on her lungs, to try and take in air, she tried to get to the head of the stairs but everything went black.

Epilogue

There was something bright behind her eyes as Magda opened them. All she could see was white and as things came into focus she realised the bright thing was a fluorescent light tube. She had no idea where she was. *Am I dead?* she thought as she looked around before realising that she was in a hospital bed. There was a button on a wire behind her head but she felt reluctant to press it. She felt so disoriented and when she tried to move her head a pain like a knife shot through it. Lifting her hands she discovered they were heavily bandaged.

Just then a woman in a blue uniform bustled in. 'Mrs. McClean you're awake! Thank the Lord.' Magda recognised the Irish accent.

'Where am I?' Her voice was thick and croaky and didn't sound like her at all.

'You're in Addenbrooke's Hospital love. You were in a nasty fire.'

'A fire?'

'Yes, in your home. Do you not remember?'

Magda didn't. It all felt as if she were in a dream.

'You were really lucky to be saved you know. You must have a guardian angel somewhere. A man saw and pulled you out I believe.'

Her words loosened something in her mind. *It was Max* she thought.

'My dogs?' She heard the rising panic in her voice.

'Oh yes, the wee dogs are fine. Your friend is looking after them. You've not been short of visitors either. Very popular you are. Now would you be havin' a little sip of water?'

The nurse handed Magda a cup with a plastic straw attached. As she lifted her head the pain shot through it again but she was so thirsty she had to have a drink. Greedily she finished the cup.

'There now, that's better is it not?'

The nurse's accent brought back Dennis so fiercely that Magda began to cry.

'There, there pet, you're safe now. You were lucky too, no burns to your lovely face, well not much. Just a big of singeing of your hair, but your hands were not so lucky. Would you be wantin' some more pain relief now? Right well I'll be gettin' you some. You sit tight now.'

As she bustled out Magda noticed a figure by the door.

'Are you ready for your first visitors?' The nurse called back over her shoulder. 'There's two young gentlemen wantin' to see you're all right.'

The visitors turned out to be Max followed closely by Tom from the cottage beyond the river.

'Magda, how are you?' Gently Max bent over to kiss her, smoothing a strand of hair away from her face. 'You gave us all such a fright.'

'Oh, Max thank you, thank you so much. You are a hero do you know that?' she croaked.

'What? What are you on about? I haven't done anything.'

'You got me out. The nurse said so.'

'No darling that wasn't me.'

Magda was confused. 'But the nurse…She said a man pulled me out.'

'Maybe so but it wasn't me.'

'Then who?'

Tom moved nearer the bed. 'No lass it weren't him. I was there. I saw 'ee. It were a tall chap, fair haired wearing some kind of uniform. I saw it clear as day. Soon as I heard them engines and saw the flames, I came running round. Them two little dogs of yourn was racing out like bats out of hell and he were there the man. He carried you out and put you on the ground. Then the ambulance come and took you away. I'm guessing you was unconscious, because I thought you was dead to be honest.'

Magda looked from one man to the other. She really had no idea what they were talking about. It had to have been Max who had got her out, nobody else was there.

'Anyway lass as I'm here already I can tell you what my old mate told me at Christmas. You was askin' about that cottage of yourn and he remembered it all. He were a bit older than me see, and he knew what went on. One of them airmen was seein' this girl. But sadly, he got shot down. The lass were pregnant too. So sad. She come from Italy apparently but some of the old 'uns round here took against her. They thought she was German see. Anyways, the long and the short of it, was they set fire to her cottage like, thinkin' she were some kind of spy. She and the little 'un died see. Thought you'd want to know the whole story.'

Tom seemed to run out of steam and he sank down onto the chair by her bed.

Magda's mind was buzzing. She could hardly make out any of it. 'My cottage; my lovely home?' Her eyes pleaded with Max.

'Yes, bit of damage done there I'm afraid, but you don't have to worry. Insurance will sort it all out and in the meantime you're staying with Janette. She's got the dogs too. Apparently it was the generator. Something wrong with it. Nothing you did. Something about the override mechanism.'

Magda remembered then how it had gone off the last time when she had been out to check it. She had presumed Max had been in and turned it off.

'Anyway, you're here, you're alive. You were very lucky someone was passing. I think it was early in the morning it all kicked off. Around four or five. You'll be up and about in no time. Janette and I are going to look after you. Now we better let you get some rest. I'll be back later to see you. Just going to run Tom here back home. He wanted to check you were okay. You've given all of us a real fright you know.'

With that Max kissed her gently on the cheek.

Tom got up in turn and stood by her bed. 'Tall chap he were what got you out. Tall with fair hair. Air force uniform. Jolly glad he was around to save you.'

He touched her arm lightly as he and Max made their way out, just as the cheery Irish nurse bustled in with her pain relief.

FICTION FROM APS BOOKS
(www.andrewsparke.com)

Davey J Ashfield: *Footsteps On The Teign*
Davey J Ashfield *Contracting With The Devil*
Davey J Ashfield: *A Turkey And One More Easter Egg*
Fenella Bass: *Hornbeams*
HR Beasley: *Nothing Left To Hide*
Lee Benson: *So You Want To Own An Art Gallery*
Lee Benson: *Where's Your Art gallery Now?*
Lee Benson: *Now You're The Artist...Deal With It*
TF Byrne *Damage Limitation*
Nargis Darby: *A Different Shade Of Love*
Jean Harvey: *Pandemic*
Michel Henri: *Mister Penny Whistle*
Michel Henri: *The Death Of The Duchess Of Grasmere*
Michel Henri: *Abducted By Faerie*
Amber J Hughes: *An Injection Of The Unexpected*
Hugh Lupus *An Extra Knot (Parts I-IV)*
Ian Meacheam: *An Inspector Called*
Tony Rowland: *Traitor Lodger German Spy*
Andrew Sparke: *Abuse Cocaine & Soft Furnishings*
Andrew Sparke: *Copper Trance & Motorways*
Phil Thompson: *Momentary Lapses In Concentration*
Paul C. Walsh: *A Place Between The Mountains*
Michael White: *Life Unfinished*

29769373R00097

Printed in Great
Britain
by Amazon